Junior Jedi Knights

Anakin Solo is going to his uncle Luke's Jedi Academy!
He will train to become part of the next generation of
Jedi Knights. The Force is with young Anakin. But he is
eleven years old . . . and he can't grow up fast
enough!

THE ALL-NEW, THRILLING ADVENTURES
OF THE JUNIOR JEDI KNIGHTS!
THE NEW HOPE FOR PEACE IN THE GALAXY!

**THIS BOOK ALSO CONTAINS
A PREVIEW OF
THE JUNIOR JEDI KNIGHTS'
NEXT EXCITING ADVENTURE:
*LYRIC'S WORLD***

Available from Boulevard Books

STAR WARS

Junior Jedi Knights

The Golden Globe

Nancy Richardson

BOULEVARD BOOKS, NEW YORK

STAR WARS: JUNIOR JEDI KNIGHTS
THE GOLDEN GLOBE

A Boulevard Book / published by arrangement with
Lucasfilm Ltd.

PRINTING HISTORY
Boulevard edition / October 1995

ISBN: 1-57297-035-9

BOULEVARD
Boulevard Books are published by The Berkley Publishing Group,
200 Madison Avenue, New York, New York 10016.
BOULEVARD and the "B" design
are trademarks belonging to The Berkley Publishing Group.

PRINTED IN THE UNITED STATES OF AMERICA

10   9   8   7

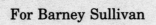

For Barney Sullivan

PROLOGUE

Nothing could have prepared him for the girl who stood before him. Her hair was pale yellow, the color of the sands of the Dune Sea on Tatooine. It moved in swirls, as if an invisible wind was stirring it. And her eyes, as they met his own ice blue ones, were the color of the green rivers that rushed across the surface of Yavin 4. There was no shyness in the smile that crinkled the corners of her eyes and made their green color dance in waves. Anakin said nothing. He was lost for a moment in the events that had brought him to this place. That had brought him to this room, and this girl.

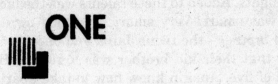

ONE

"Anakin, we'll miss you," Leia Organa Solo said to her son.

Leia and her husband, Han Solo, stood with their younger son, Anakin, by the silver shuttle that would take the boy to Yavin 4. That was the moon where Leia's brother, the Jedi Luke Skywalker, had created a Jedi academy. The academy was built to train people to become Jedi Knights, protectors of freedom and justice. Only beings who had shown they were skilled in working with the Force had been invited to attend the academy. Anakin was one of those chosen to attend the first session created for younger children and aliens.

Anakin was sensitive to the Force. He had been aware he possessed the ability to alter, understand, and control his surroundings ever since he could remember. It was just little things. Anakin

3

could feel other people's emotions if he tried really hard. He could lift small objects with his thoughts. Added to these talents was the fact that he was smart. Very smart. Even his own sister and brother—the twins Jaina and Jacen—admitted that their kid brother was a genius. By the age of five, Anakin knew how to take apart computers and put them back together. He loved any kind of puzzle, whether it was taking apart machinery and learning how to rebuild it or figuring out difficult word games with his mind.

When Anakin turned eleven years old his parents agreed it was time for him to attend the Jedi academy. Anakin showed too much ability to be kept at home. When Jaina and Jacen returned from their time at the academy, his parents agreed to send their younger son there to study. Leia wouldn't have been able to bear sending all of her children to Yavin 4 at one time. She would have missed them too much. Jaina and Jacen had now returned. It was Anakin's turn to leave.

Leia studied her younger son. Anakin was about 150 centimeters tall. He was slender and had brown hair that constantly fell into his eyes. He had Luke's eyes—ice blue and full of strength and curiosity. But his quiet nature and concentration came from his mother. Leia smiled. Perhaps her younger son would grow up to help rule the New Republic, as she did. Or perhaps he would become a starship pilot and a Rebel hero like his father, Han Solo. If Anakin did grow up to be like his father, Leia wouldn't have a moment's peace, she knew. She would always worry about the trouble Anakin might be in.

But for now Anakin would live on Yavin 4, a safe, quiet moon orbiting the giant gas planet Yavin. Leia knew that her brother Luke would take care of his nephew. Still, she couldn't help worrying about her child. She sensed that the Force was very strong within him. And while she was proud of his power, she worried that it might lead him into danger. Anyone who had the power to become a Jedi and use the Force for good also ran the risk of being lured into using the Force for evil and personal gain—that was the dark side of the Force.

Leia watched Anakin say good-bye to his brother and sister. She almost wished that Anakin had a twin too. That way he wouldn't be alone on Yavin 4. Her younger son did not have many friends. His brother and sister and the droid See-Threepio were really his closest companions.

"Stop worrying, Leia," Han said to his wife. He could hear her worry as clearly as if she'd spoken. "Come here, kiddo, and say good-bye to your old dad," Han called to his son. Anakin came over to hug his father. Han ruffled his son's hair. Then he brushed it out of Anakin's eyes.

"I'll be fine, Dad," Anakin said. He could feel his father's worry, just as he could feel his mother's.

His kid was so strong, Han thought. But for a moment he, too, worried about the power of the Force in Anakin. Then Leia pulled her son into a tight hug.

"Call us if you need anything," Leia said. Or if you want to come home, Leia thought.

"I promise," Anakin answered his mother. Then he stepped inside the shuttle and waved to his family from the window by his seat. Anakin was all alone now. He settled back into his chair to think.

Anakin thought about his parents and their fears. What they didn't understand was that their younger son had not been afraid to leave his home planet of Coruscant. Anakin had seen the look of worry in his mother's eyes as she and his father had said good-bye to him. But Anakin wasn't worried. He was traveling to Yavin 4, where Uncle Luke had created a Jedi academy to train the young who were gifted in the Jedi ways. Anakin knew that just as his twin brother and sister Jacen and Jaina were sensitive to the Force, he was too.

No, Anakin wasn't afraid, but he was silent during the journey to Yavin 4. There would be so much to learn in the next few months, and Anakin wanted to think about what lay ahead.

"We'll be landing in five minutes," the shuttle

commander informed his young charge. Anakin turned, his ice blue eyes peering out the window, making a sweep of Yavin 4's surface. He'd read all about the moon. Still, its lush jungles, rivers, and waterfalls took his breath away. It was so unlike the city he had just left. So beautiful and wild. With an impatient toss of his head he swept long dark bangs from his eyes as the shuttle dove toward an enormous stone structure. Anakin knew that this was the Great Temple, an ancient building that had been on Yavin 4 long before Luke Skywalker had chosen it for his Jedi academy. There were several other temples and palaces on the moon, but most were falling apart. It was said that some were more than four thousand years old. Anakin wondered if he would have the chance to explore those buildings. He hoped so.

# TWO

Once the silver shuttle was safely settled on the Great Temple's landing field, its door opened with a hiss. Anakin walked onto the launch bay and into the waiting arms of his uncle, the Jedi Master Luke Skywalker. Luke wore a black jumpsuit. His hair was a few shades lighter than Anakin's. But his eyes were the same bright blue.

"Anakin, welcome to the academy," Luke said with a smile. Anakin hugged his uncle, then bent to say hello to Luke's companion, the silver, blue, and white droid Artoo-Detoo. Artoo's red lights blipped and beeped at the boy, but Anakin couldn't understand anything the droid was saying. "He says he's glad that you're finally here," Luke explained.

Over the next few hours Luke showed Anakin around the academy and told its history. "The Great Temple was one of many palaces built by

9

the Massassi," Luke explained. "They were a race of people who once lived on Yavin 4. They disappeared from the moon long before it was discovered by the Rebel Alliance." Anakin knew what the Rebel Alliance was. It was the name for the men, women, and aliens who had fought to bring back justice and freedom to the galaxy. His mother, father, and Uncle Luke had been part of that group.

"The Great Temple was renovated years ago by the Alliance and used as a secret base," Luke explained. "Then it was found by the Death Star and abandoned." The Death Star, Anakin remembered, was the battle station of the Empire. That was the Rebel Alliance's enemy. "When the Death Star found the Alliance base on Yavin 4, a war followed. Some of the temples on this planet were damaged by crashing TIE fighters, but the years have also taken their toll on them. However, the Great Temple was undamaged, so we decided to use it for the Jedi academy," Luke said.

Anakin ran his fingers along the stone blocks that lined the hallways of the academy. He wondered what the Great Temple had looked like long ago, and what the Massassi people had been like.

"The Great Temple hasn't been changed much on the outside," Luke said. He had sensed his nephew's curiosity. "But we had to change the inside in order to create the academy rooms. We've divided some spaces into sleeping and refresher units for you and your classmates. And we've hung heavy drapes above the open windows. The windows in the Temple have no glass because the climate here is so warm that we rarely need it. However, every few months we have terrible storms. The temperature drops and rain and winds whip through the jungle. When that happens the heavy drapes keep the temple warm and dry. There's one place that we haven't touched, though—the Grand Audience Chamber at the top of the Temple. All of the instructors and students here agree that it is just too beautiful to change," Luke explained.

Luke and his newest student continued to walk through the academy. Every few minutes Luke stopped to introduce Anakin to his Jedi instructors. "Anakin, this is Tionne," Luke said when they stopped before a silver-haired humanoid woman with enormous pearl-colored eyes. Anakin shook Tionne's hand. "Tionne is a Jedi Knight and she also loves to collect old Jedi legends and songs," Luke told the boy. "Come on, I'll introduce you to some of your fellow students," Luke offered. "You were the last to arrive for this session of the academy."

The two went through a large wooden doorway and entered the dining room. Luke walked his nephew from table to table, making introductions. Anakin had rarely seen so many different creatures under one roof. There were aliens of all different colors—red, green, purple. Some had bodies like birds, others looked like snakes, and some had eight or ten arms and several eyes.

"There are many beings who are sensitive to the Force," Luke explained to his nephew. "Whether they are human or alien is not important. The only thing that matters is that everyone in this room is dedicated to becoming a Jedi Knight and using the Force for good."

This is going to take some getting used to, Anakin thought as he scanned the room. But making friends wasn't Anakin's biggest concern. He was a loner, and even at home his only close friends were his brother and sister and Threepio. No, he was at the academy to learn how to understand and use the Force—an energy field binding all living things. That was what gave Jedi Knights their power. And more than anything else, Anakin wanted to be a Jedi Knight. Not just because his brother and sister were training to be Jedi, although he had been jealous when they had left to study at the Jedi academy months before. No, Anakin wanted to be a Jedi Knight because he knew in his heart that he had been born to be a Jedi Knight.

By dinnertime Anakin had met so many new people that his head was spinning. All he wanted was some time for himself. But he could not escape from the rest of the students until after dinner. At one point he tried to sneak out of the dining hall, but Tionne saw him, and just as he was about to slip away, Anakin felt her hand on his shoulder.

"Do not be so shy," she said gently.

Anakin had to bite his lip to keep from telling the silver-haired humanoid the truth. He wasn't shy; that was a mistake even his mother and father made. He just liked to spend time by himself —time thinking. Anakin made a note that the first thing he would have to do was to learn the best times to sneak away from the group. Finally dinner ended, and Anakin set off to explore the Temple by himself.

"Bleep, bleep."

Oh no, Anakin thought, and stopped in his tracks. He turned to see Artoo-Detoo scooting up behind him. "Go back to Uncle Luke," Anakin commanded the droid. Artoo came to a halt before him, bleeping once. "I don't know what you're saying but I want to be alone," Anakin said. Artoo still did not turn to leave. "Okay, you can come with me, but please don't make any noise. I want to think," explained Anakin. Artoo was silent. At least he understands me, Anakin said to himself as he began to walk down a long stone hall.

"Bink, bleep, bobeep."

Anakin shook his head, but kept walking. "Artoo, we have got to learn how to communicate if you are going to follow me around," he grumbled at the droid.

Anakin came to the base of a stone stairway at the end of a long corridor. "These stairs will be too difficult for you to climb, Artoo—guess this is where we part company," Anakin said to the droid with a sly smile. Then he turned and began to climb the stairs, gently running his fingertips along walls that narrowed as he moved upward. At the top of the stairway was a large wooden doorway, different from the doors that dotted the halls of the Temple. It was carved with symbols Anakin didn't recognize—shapes that curved and twirled in a beautiful pattern. Anakin had reached the Grand Audience Chamber. It was the highest room in the Temple, and unlike the other rooms, it had not been rebuilt for the academy.

Gently Anakin pushed open the large doors. He walked into the center of the Grand Audience Chamber. The walls were a deep tan stone, worn smooth over the years. Blueleaf shrubs, the most common shrub on the moon, poked through several cracks in the stones. They attached themselves to the stone with suckers. The shrubs were electric blue, and as Anakin leaned close he could smell a spicy perfume. He walked slowly toward a large window. The view was breathtaking. Anakin looked down on the jungle. It was carpeted with blueleaf, and filled with Massassi trees whose bark shone purplish brown. Weaving through the trees, he could see sparkling green rivers that rushed along the moon. Beautiful, Anakin thought.

"Who are you?" a voice sang out behind Anakin.

Anakin whirled. A young girl stood before him. Pale yellow hair, green eyes, an orange academy jumpsuit, and bare feet. "Bantha got your tongue?" she giggled as she moved to Anakin's side by the window. She couldn't have been more than ten years old, Anakin thought.

"My name is Tahiri and I'm nine years old," the girl sang out in a voice that sounded like a bubbling stream. Anakin didn't reply. He was annoyed that she had interrupted his thoughts. Annoyed that she had found the Grand Audience Chamber.

"Where are your shoes?" Anakin finally said to break the silence.

"I don't wear any—never, not ever," Tahiri began. "I'm from Tatooine. I'm one of the Sand People." Anakin's jaw dropped down in wonder. He had never seen one of the Sand People without their heavy robes and the strips of cloth, breath masks, and eye protectors they wore over their face, and didn't know anyone who had. Tatooine was a harsh desert planet, and the people needed all the protection from the sand, sun, and wind they could wear.

"Well, I'm not actually one of the Sand People, but I've lived with them since I was four years old," Tahiri continued. "I was an orphan, and they found me in the desert and took care of me." She moved to the large wooden bench by the window and perched on it. Then she resumed her story.

"Luke Skywalker's assistant, Tionne, discovered me while she and Luke were visiting Tatooine. They spent time with me and discovered that I'm strong in the Force. I didn't know what they meant at first. But they explained that the little things I could do—like sense emotions and find things that were misplaced—were a special power. So Tionne rescued me from the desert and brought me to this moon. Not that I needed rescue. The Sand People are all right, and I did have my own bantha as a pet—you have seen a bantha, haven't you?" Tahiri asked Anakin. She didn't wait for an answer. "Banthas are animals with long, thick fur. They have spiral horns. On Tatooine we ride them and use them to carry things. Anyway, Tionne brought me here because she says that I have Jedi potential. Guess that's why you're here too, huh?" Once again Tahiri did not wait for an answer. "Best thing about this place is that I don't have to wear long white robes and cover my face and mouth like I did on Tatooine—I hated that! Oh, and I don't ever have to wear shoes if I don't want to—I made Tionne promise me that the moment I arrived at the Great Temple," Tahiri explained, wriggling her bare feet. "I made her promise because I love the feeling of the Temple's cool clean stones under my

feet. Where I'm from it's hot and there's sand everywhere—gritty sand that sticks between your
toes. So, aren't you going to say something?" she
finally asked Anakin.

Anakin had to laugh. "It's pretty hard to get a
word in with you talking all the time," he explained.

Tahiri thought for a moment. "Sorry about that.
It's just that on Tatooine there wasn't anyone
near my own age to talk to. I guess I'm pretty
lonely for a friend."

"I guess I could use a friend too," Anakin admitted. After all, his brother and sister were back on
Coruscant with their parents, and Anakin already missed them, more than he could say.

"Then it's settled—we're best friends now,"
Tahiri said with a grin. "So are you going to tell
me your name?"

"My name is Anakin Solo," he replied softly.

THREE

Jedi instructor Tionne found her newest student, Tahiri, in the Grand Audience Chamber. She had come to take the girl to her sleeping quarters. There had not been a chance to show the active young student where she was to sleep since the girl had arrived on the moon that morning. For the last few hours Tionne had had a hard enough time just keeping her eye on this last-minute addition to the young Jedi class, a class that had been carefully selected and then brought to Yavin 4 over the last week for classes that would begin tomorrow morning.

Tionne walked through the wooden doorway and paused, watching Tahiri talk to Anakin Solo. Tionne was happy to see that the child had begun to make a friend. She had known that Tahiri wasn't shy. In fact, the girl rarely stopped talking. But Tionne had been worried that the other

19

students would be put off by her nonstop chatter. It was understandable, though, since the girl hadn't had any human her own age to talk to for almost six years. "Tahiri, I've come to show you to your room," Tionne said.

Tahiri looked away from her new friend and toward the silver-haired Jedi. "I'm not tired. I want to stay and talk with Anakin," Tahiri replied. Tahiri wasn't used to anyone telling her when to sleep, or where. On Tatooine everyone took care of themselves. If you were tired you slept. If you were hungry you ate. And if you were thirsty . . . Well, if you were thirsty you hoped to find water somewhere in the desert.

Tionne smiled at Tahiri. "You are not on Tatooine anymore," she said. "And you will follow the rules of the Jedi academy." Tahiri frowned and her bright green eyes clouded. She really did hate being told what to do. But she stood up from the bench. She would follow Tionne for now.

"Young Anakin, it is almost time for lights out," Tionne informed the boy. "All of our young students must be in their rooms and ready for bed four standard hours after nightfall," she continued. Anakin nodded. He was used to being told when to go to bed. On Coruscant his mother and father had made him go to bed at about the same time.

Anakin, Tahiri, and Tionne left the Grand Audience Chamber and descended the stairway to the next floor of the Temple. Artoo was still waiting at the base of the stairs for Anakin, and when the boy reached the bottom of the stairs the droid once again followed him. Several times he bleeped and beeped, but Anakin ignored the droid. "Well, this is my room," Anakin said softly when he reached a door. "Good night, everyone." He pushed open a large wooden door and entered the room.

"This way, Tahiri," Tionne said. The two continued down the hallway until they reached another door. "This is your room. When you hear the wake-up bell tomorrow morning please use your refresher unit to clean up and then come down to the dining room." Tahiri scowled, then stepped inside the room.

Tahiri stood with her back to the wooden door. She had never had her own room before. On the planet Tatooine all of the Sand People slept outdoors in encampments on blankets on the ground. Now Tahiri was looking around her very own room. She couldn't believe it!

There was a large sleeping pad in the far corner, covered with soft white blankets. A dresser and a closet were on the wall to her left. Several orange jumpsuits hung from hooks in the closet. There was also one pair of shoes on the floor. No chance I'm going to wear those, Tahiri thought as she looked at the shoes. She walked toward another doorway directly across from her bed. It led

to her very own refresher unit. I can't believe this
place, she thought.

Tahiri had never even had a shower before
she'd left Tatooine. There was barely enough water to drink on the planet. A shower was unheard-
of! Luke and Tionne had made Tahiri take one on
their shuttle. She smiled. The way they had wrinkled their noses when she had unwrapped herself
from the white robe she wore had been funny. She
must have really smelled awful. Tahiri had to admit she'd liked the warm shower. And she liked
the orange jumpsuit they'd given her even more.
It was so much more comfortable than her robe
had been.

Tahiri rubbed her feet along the cool stone floor.
The clean stones felt wonderful. She changed into
her nightgown, raced across the floor, and leapt
onto her bed. Tahiri sank into the blankets. So
soft and fluffy, she thought dreamily. Maybe she
was ready to sleep after all, she thought right before she drifted off.

Tahiri began to dream. It was the exact same
dream she'd had on Tatooine. The same dream
she'd had every few weeks of her life for as long as
she could remember. She was floating along a
green river in a long silver raft with rounded
sides. Before Tahiri had come to Yavin 4 she had
never even seen a river. Strange to have imagined
something I've never seen, she thought in her
dream.

Tahiri could feel the cold water lap her hands as she paddled in the raft. A storm was brewing. The wind was growing stronger, and the water began to hit the sides of the raft in powerful waves. Tahiri paddled harder, her muscles beginning to ache. She had to reach the side of the river before her raft was turned over by the swell. A giant wave swept over the front of the raft. Tahiri was hit full force, and her small body was sent flying backward. She fell from the raft and was quickly swept into the cold river water.

This was the part where she usually woke up. But not this time.

This time Tahiri felt the waves tumbling over her, smacking her face and filling her nose and mouth with water. She could feel herself desperately struggling to breathe. Why hadn't she woken up? She thrashed through the water trying to get back to her raft. She could still see it above the tumbling waves. And then she saw him. It was the boy she'd just met. Anakin Solo was in her raft. And he was paddling toward her. He held a silver paddle out. It rose and fell from her vision as she was carried along wave after wave.

Tahiri knew that she was supposed to reach for the paddle, that if she didn't she would surely drown. But she couldn't grab it. It was too far away. She saw Anakin screaming at her, but she couldn't hear his words. The water was swallowing her up. And then suddenly the cold silver paddle was within reach and she was again grabbing for it. But just as her fingers began to close over it a loud bell sounded.

Tahiri awoke with a start. Strange, she thought groggily, I've had the same dream on Tatooine ever since I was a small child, but the dream usually ends when I fall into the river. I've never almost drowned, or been saved by a boy. There has never been anyone else on the river with me.

Tahiri dropped her feet over the side of her pad and stood. Her nightgown clung to her body in sweaty spots. Yuck, she thought, and headed to the refresher unit.

In my dream I was on Yavin 4, Tahiri thought as she showered. In fact, it looked like the river that runs by the academy. But where was I going? And why was Anakin Solo in my dream? Tahiri wondered. "I think I should get to know my new friend Anakin better if he's going to turn up in a dream I've been having my whole life," Tahiri muttered as she slipped on her jumpsuit. She opened her door and headed to the dining room, determined to understand her strange dream.

FOUR

"We need to talk, Anakin," Tahiri said as she arrived at the morning meal and sat down at the breakfast table beside her new best friend.

Anakin wasn't a morning person. "Oh hi," he said with a grumble as Tahiri sat across from him. "Look, I don't like to talk in the morning," he tried to explain.

"Nonsense. You don't like to talk period," Tahiri replied. "Last night I did all the talking. Now I want to know a little bit about you." Tahiri wasn't ready to tell him about the dream. That would have to wait until she could be sure that he wouldn't laugh at her. She hated to be laughed at. "Go on," she prodded when Anakin still hadn't spoken.

"You're not going to leave me alone no matter what I say, are you?" Anakin asked grumpily. Tahiri just stared at him, her green eyes glowing.

Anakin hated telling people about himself. He swallowed, then quickly began to recite his family history.

"My mother and father are famous. My mom is Leia Organa Solo and she's a princess from the planet Alderaan and chief of state of the New Republic. Both she and my father, Han Solo, were Rebel heroes. My uncle is Luke Skywalker, the famous Jedi Master and the founder of this academy. The entire family is almost too much to live up to." Anakin growled. "Okay, are you satisfied now?"

"You don't have to live up to them," Tahiri said matter-of-factly. "You aren't them and they aren't you."

"Easy for you to say," Anakin replied.

"I would rather have a family than not have one at all," Tahiri shot back.

"I thought your family were the Sand People," Anakin said.

"They are, but not really," Tahiri answered. "The Sand People found me in the desert. But my real parents were moisture farmers on Tatooine. My parents had machines that pulled water from the air. That water was used on the planet for drinking and farming. I don't really remember them. The Sand People said they were killed when I was four. I'm not sure how they died, though."

"I'm sorry," Anakin said.

"Don't feel sorry for me," Tahiri replied fiercely. "I'm lucky that the Sand People found me in the desert. Just like I'm lucky that Luke and Tionne found me on Tatooine."

"You're right," Anakin agreed. He was beginning to feel more at ease with Tahiri. He took another bite of food, then said, "I even have an older brother and sister. They're 13 years old and their names are Jacen and Jaina."

"What are they like?" Tahiri asked her friend.

"Well, Jacen is pretty wild. He loves spending time outside. He collects bugs and gets into a lot of trouble. Jaina is more like me. She likes taking things apart and then figuring out how to put them together. I don't get to spend too much time with either of them. They were on Yavin 4 for the past few months studying. Now I'm here," Anakin explained.

"You miss them, don't you," Tahiri said.

"Yeah. They're my best friends," Anakin admitted.

"Well, now you have me," Tahiri said with a quick grin. "And I have something I need to tell you. Last night I had a dream—the same dream I've had most of my life for as long as I can remember. It's a strange dream. Strange, because in it I'm rafting on a river, and before yesterday I'd never seen a river. In fact, before I came to this moon I'd never seen so much water in my life. Anyway, I'm pretty sure that this dream I've been having has always taken place here, on Yavin 4. Which is truly weird, don't you think, because this is my first time here." Tahiri didn't wait for Anakin's comments.

"Anyway, in the dream I'm always rafting a river when a terrible storm begins. The winds howl and the water of the river grows into giant waves. One of the waves hits me and I'm thrown out of the raft. That's when I usually wake up. But last night I didn't wake up. Instead I almost drowned. I didn't, though, because the breakfast bell rang and I was woken up. But that's not important right now. What's important is that for the first time in all the years that I can remember dreaming this exact same dream, someone else was in it too. That someone was in my raft, and when I was swept into the river he held out a silver paddle to save me from drowning. The boy who held out that paddle was you!"

Anakin was silent. So this was what his brother Jacen was always talking about. I guess girls do get crushes on boys and say things that make no sense, he thought.

"Aren't you going to say anything?" Tahiri asked impatiently.

"Well, I don't think it's so strange that you had a dream with me in it," Anakin began. "After all, we met last night right before you went to sleep."

"Don't flatter yourself. You're not so terrific that I'd have a dream about you for no reason," Tahiri retorted, her irritation showing in her flashing eyes.

Now she's upset with me, Anakin thought with wonder. "Don't be annoyed, Tahiri," he said. "I just thought that might be one explanation."

"And what about the river, the storm, and the fact that my dream has always taken place here, on this moon, when I've lived in the desert all my life?" Tahiri asked in exasperation.

"Well, you said yourself that you can hardly remember anything about your life before the Sand People adopted you. Maybe you've been here before," Anakin suggested.

"Been where?" Luke Skywalker asked his newest student as he walked up behind her. Tahiri whirled around to face the Jedi Master.

"Nowhere," Tahiri huffed. She kicked back her chair and stalked from the table.

"Making friends so soon, young Anakin?" Luke asked with a smile. Anakin gave a feeble grin and then he, too, rose and left the table. He wanted to find Tahiri to apologize for whatever he'd done wrong. The girl talked too much, but she was his new friend and he didn't want to hurt her feelings.

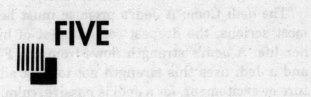

FIVE

There was no time for Anakin to talk to Tahiri before the bell rang for the first class of the Junior Jedi Academy. Anakin walked into the Grand Audience Chamber and looked for her. He spotted her blonde hair in the third row and quickly slid in beside her. Tahiri pretended not to see him. Anakin tried to apologize, but she just stared at the large block walls to her left. Guess I'll try later, Anakin thought.

The large assembly hall walls were dark green blocks of stone. Polished wooden benches were set in rows. In the front of the room was a small platform. The students filed into the rows. They spoke quietly as they waited for Luke Skywalker to enter the room. Some had never heard the Jedi Master speak. But even those who had were excited. Luke Skywalker was their hero. Luke walked silently into the room. He stepped onto the platform and began to speak to the newest and youngest class of the Jedi academy.

"The Jedi Code: A Jedi's promise must be the most serious, the deepest commitment of his or her life. A Jedi's strength flows from the Force, and a Jedi uses this strength not to seek adventure or excitement, for a Jedi is passive, calm, and at peace," Luke explained.

The room was quiet as Luke Skywalker spoke. Tahiri even stopped running her bare feet along the smooth classroom floor. Anakin could feel the excitement in the room. Each of the twenty Jedi candidates was thrilled by Luke's words.

"A Jedi knows that anger, fear, and aggression lead to the dark side," continued Luke. "A Jedi uses the Force for knowledge and defense, never for attack. For a Jedi there is no 'try,' only 'do.' Believe and you succeed. Above all else, know that control of the Force comes only from concentration and training."

Luke Skywalker stopped speaking and stood studying the students. He met each one's gaze, pausing for a moment when he reached Anakin. He could already sense the power of the Force in the boy. It was so strong for one so young, he said to himself. Luke understood Leia and Han's worry. When the Force was strong it attracted attention from evil men and women, who might want to use Anakin to serve the dark side. He would have to keep a sharp eye on his nephew. Then Luke moved on to Tahiri.

He had a special place in his heart for the young girl. Tahiri was from Luke's home planet of Tatooine. Luke had been a farm boy, raised by his aunt and uncle, Owen and Beru Lars. Luke had hated the desert planet. It was so hot and dry, and he had been bored—that is, until he met two droids that his uncle had purchased. Their names were See-Threepio and Artoo-Detoo. The droids had come to Tatooine in search of the Jedi Master Obi-Wan Kenobi. They had a message for him from Princess Leia of Alderaan. She was being held prisoner by Darth Vader. Vader was an evil man who was overseeing construction of the Death Star—the Empire's battle station.

Luke followed Artoo-Detoo to Obi-Wan, and the Jedi told Luke about his family. Obi-Wan said that Luke's father had been a Jedi Knight and had been killed. Obi-Wan promised to train Luke. And that was how his life as a Jedi Knight had begun.

Luke looked at Tahiri. She was an orphan. Although no details were known about their deaths, her parents had been killed on Tatooine. Tahiri had been raised by the Sand People as their own. But Luke understood that Tahiri had never been one of the Sand People. She had been just as bored on Tatooine as he had been. On a recent trip to the planet, he and the Jedi Knight Tionne had immediately sensed the power of the Force within her. Tahiri was meant to be a Jedi Knight, Luke knew. But he also knew that someday Tahiri would have to make a choice. He had promised the Sand People that he would return Tahiri to Tatooine when she was ready to decide whether she wanted to remain with them or continue her training as a Jedi Knight. Luke hoped that she would choose to stay at the academy, but that would be her decision.

"You are all here because the power of the Force is strong within you," Luke said firmly. "You are here because the New Republic needs Jedi Knights. And you are here because it is your destiny to train to become Jedi Knights and use the Force when necessary to maintain peace in our galaxy. Over the next month your instructors will begin to train you to see the Force in everything around you. You will learn to use the Force to see far-off places, defend yourselves, and do things you never believed possible. Just remember that the Force must never be used in anger or aggression. Otherwise you will be serving the dark side, the evil side." The room remained silent.

"I want to tell you about the dark side," Luke said softly. "Because if you understand it, you will not be drawn to it. When I was a boy I was told that my father had been a Jedi Knight. I was told that he had been killed by an evil man named

Darth Vader. Darth Vader was a man who helped build the Death Star created by Emperor Palpatine in order to control the galaxy through fear and violence. I met Darth Vader in a battle on Cloud City. It was during this battle that I learned that my father had not been killed by Vader. My father *was* Darth Vader." Anakin could hear his friend Tahiri gasp. He wondered if he was the only student in the room who already knew this entire story.

"My father had once been a man named Anakin Skywalker. He was an expert pilot. He was trained as a Jedi Knight by Obi-Wan Kenobi. My father understood the Force. But he chose to use it to gain power. That choice turned him to the dark side—the place where a Jedi's powers are used in anger. You all know that Darth Vader and the Emperor almost destroyed the Rebellion. If they had won, none of you would be here now. If they had won, the entire galaxy would be run by evil men and women. That is the power of the dark side of the Force. Remember it." Luke closed his eyes and took a deep breath before he continued.

"As new candidates it is important that you understand the rules of the academy. Above all, you are here to study. Since you are the youngest class ever to come to this moon, we have imposed several rules for your safety. No one is to leave this area without permission. Although Yavin 4 is quiet and peaceful, it can be a dangerous place. In addition, you are all from different worlds and have different ways of living. That means that you will have to get used to each other. There is to be no fighting among you. Patience and understanding are important skills for Jedi candidates to learn. Failure to follow the rules of the academy may result in your being sent home." He paused, then said, "Now it is time to begin. Please follow the instructors to your classrooms." The students rose and filed from the room; some scooted on eight legs, some walked, and several of the birdlike creatures hopped.

"Did you catch that word, 'destiny'?" Tahiri whispered to Anakin as they left the room.

"Shhh, I'm thinking," Anakin whispered back. He didn't tell her that he was thinking about his own name. He had been named after Luke and Leia's father. He had been named after Anakin Skywalker, who was Darth Vader. He tried to remember that his uncle Luke had finally been able to reach the good buried inside Vader. That in a battle between the light and dark side of the Force, Luke's father had turned against the dark side to save his son's life. Still, Anakin was a scary name.

Tahiri ignored Anakin and continued to whisper. "Anakin, the word 'destiny' means to do something you are meant to do. I have this weird feeling that destiny has brought you and me together. I know you're not going to like this, but I think we are meant to raft the river on Yavin 4. That's why you were in my dream last night. I think we should sneak out of the academy and go raft the river."

"What?" Anakin said. "Are you crazy? We just got here. We're here to learn about the Force, to become Jedi Knights. If we sneak out we might get into trouble. And if that happens my parents would be told." Anakin had a brief flash of their disappointed faces. He could just hear Jacen and Jaina scolding him. "No way," he whispered fiercely to Tahiri. There was no way this girl was going to get Anakin to disappoint his family or risk the chance that his uncle might decide he was too much trouble to have at the academy. No way.

That night the dream came. Anakin knew it was the same one Tahiri had spoken about. But instead of Tahiri, it was Anakin who sat inside a long silver raft. In his hand was a silver paddle and he was leaning over the rounded side of the raft, stroking the cold green water. It lapped over his hands until they felt like ice, but he continued to paddle.

Where am I going? Anakin wondered. He stared at the giant trees that hung over the river. He recognized them as being from Yavin 4—they were Massassi trees, their bark a purplish brown. But where was the storm Tahiri had told him about? Almost in answer to his question, Anakin heard a rumbling from behind him. He looked over his shoulder and saw a massive black cloud rolling through the sky toward him.

He began to paddle harder. He had to get to the side of the river before the storm hit. His arms ached with effort. The water began to strike his raft in waves and the wind almost tore the paddle from his icy hands. This dream seems so real, Anakin thought wildly as he struggled to reach the shore. The wind whipped his hair into his face and he almost didn't see her. It was her orange jumpsuit that caught his eye.

Tahiri was in the rapids in front of him. She was struggling to keep her head above the waves. Anakin desperately paddled toward his friend. He tried to shout to her but he couldn't even hear his own voice above the storm. And then Tahiri saw him. For a split second Anakin's ice blue eyes met her frightened green ones. He watched as Tahiri struggled toward the paddle he held out to her. She kept getting swept beneath the swells. Swim, Anakin screamed in his mind. Tahiri's hand shot toward the paddle and her fingers closed around it, then slipped away. She was swept out of sight beneath the wild water. Anakin leapt from side to side in the raft trying to spot Tahiri beneath the swells. He had lost her. Then he heard a soft sound in the distance and realized it was the academy wake-up bell. The river slowly faded before his eyes.

Anakin walked down the corridor to the dining room. He wasn't ready to talk to Tahiri about his dream. He wasn't ready to admit that maybe his friend was right, that maybe something was pulling them both to that river. Whether or not it was destiny Anakin wasn't sure. But he did know that he didn't want to have the dream again. It had been terrifying.

SIX

"You look terrible," Tahiri sang out to Anakin as he sat down at the dining hall table beside her. And he did. There were deep purple circles beneath his eyes. Anakin looked like he hadn't slept a wink. "Trouble sleeping?" Tahiri asked as she stuffed her mouth with a roll. Anakin was silent.

Tahiri turned to face her friend squarely. "Are you still mad about my idea of going rafting?" she whispered. No answer. "Well, don't be. For the first time that I can remember I didn't have a dream about the river last night. Maybe telling you about it broke some sort of cycle. Now I'm free," she said with a giggle. "So don't worry, we don't have to sneak out of the academy, and I'm sorry for suggesting such a risky idea."

"Yes we do," Anakin replied.

Now it was Tahiri's turn to fall silent. Finally

she sputtered, "What in the name of the Great Bantha are you talking about?"

"The reason you didn't have that dream last night is because I did," Anakin replied softly as he stared at his uneaten meal. "I dreamt I was in a raft on the river, and it was just like you said, only I was the one paddling and you weren't there. At least not until later."

"What happened later?" Tahiri said under her breath. She wondered if Anakin could sense the fear in her voice.

"You drowned," Anakin quietly replied. "I tried to save you," he added, "but the river was too strong. I'm sorry." Anakin hung his head. He was ashamed he hadn't been able to save his friend. It was only a dream, he knew, but he also knew it was more than that. Tahiri was staring at him. She looked scared. "You don't have to go with me to the river, Tahiri," Anakin said. "But I feel like I'm being pulled there and I think I've got to go see why."

"Why don't we talk to your uncle Luke about this? Maybe he should come with us," Tahiri suggested.

"No!" Anakin cried. It was the first time Tahiri had heard him speak in a voice much above a whisper. "We can't tell Luke Skywalker. If we do then everything will be lost," Anakin said fiercely.

"What are you talking about, Anakin?" Tahiri asked.

"I don't know," Anakin replied in a surprised voice. "But when you suggested we talk to Uncle Luke I heard a voice inside my head. It said that we can't tell Uncle Luke or everything will be lost."

"What will be lost?" Tahiri asked.

"I don't know," Anakin said with a look of frustration. This was not what he wanted. He was on Yavin 4 to study. To become a Jedi Knight. Now there was a strange voice inside his head telling him to keep something from his uncle Luke. Telling him to sneak out of the academy to raft a river. And the worst part was that he believed in the voice, felt that what it said to him was right. More than that, he believed that the voice came from a Jedi Master. In it, he had heard a strength and calm that was similar to his uncle's voice. Perhaps this unknown Jedi Master needed Anakin to perform an important task, a task that would pave the way for his becoming a Jedi Knight. But what if he was wrong about the voice? What if he was being drawn to the dark side of the Force? What if, he wondered, it's calling me just as it did my grandfather Anakin Skywalker?

There was only one way to find out.

"I guess I better start figuring when to sneak out of the academy," Anakin mumbled.

"You mean *we* better," Tahiri said with a grin. "And don't worry, if we get kicked out of the academy—not that I think we will—you can come home with me."

"And be one of the Sand People?" Anakin replied with a little laugh. "Thanks, but no thanks." Anakin fell silent. He wasn't sure he should let Tahiri come with him to the river. After all, she had drowned in his dream. "Tahiri, maybe you shouldn't get involved in this," Anakin began.

"I know that you're worried about me drowning," Tahiri replied. "But I have to come with you. We've both had the dream, and that means we're both supposed to raft the river. Something is calling to us, Anakin," Tahiri said in a faltering voice. "And even though I'm scared, I'm going with you."

"The raft will be at the edge of the river," Anakin whispered to Tahiri the following morning across their class desks.

"How do you know that?" Tahiri whispered back.

"I just know—that same voice, the one that told me we can't talk to Uncle Luke about our dream, told me last night," Anakin replied. He stared in frustration at Tahiri. She wanted answers that he just didn't have. Last night, right before he'd fallen into the same dream, he'd heard the voice. It told him not to worry. That the raft he and Tahiri needed would be at the edge of the river. That they should both sneak out of the academy and go to the raft.

"What if the voice is evil?" Tahiri whispered in a frightened voice. "What if we're being pulled to use the Force to seek adventure and excitement instead of using it for calm and peace like your uncle Luke warned? I don't want to serve the dark side like Darth Vader did—"

"Are you saying that because Darth Vader was my grandfather?" Anakin asked in an insulted voice. "Because if you can't trust me then you shouldn't come with me." Anakin couldn't meet Tahiri's eyes when he said these words. He was afraid. Afraid that Tahiri saw some evil in him. Something that made him the same as his grandfather.

"No, Anakin, I didn't mean that you are anything like Darth Vader. It's just that we're trusting some strange voice inside your head," Tahiri explained. "How do we know that the voice is good?"

"I just know, Tahiri," Anakin replied in a trembling voice. "And I'm going to figure out a way to sneak out of the academy in the next few days."

Tahiri stared at her friend. She understood why Anakin was so upset. It wasn't just the voice in his head. If he got caught, she knew, a lot of people would be disappointed in him. His mother and father, his brother and sister. Luke Skywalker. Tahiri didn't have to worry about anyone caring whether or not she was sent home. That made it easier to take the risk. Still, Anakin was driving her crazy. She fixed her friend with an irritated look.

"Is there a problem here?" instructor Tionne asked her students as she walked up to their desks.

"No problem," Anakin replied. "Except that neither of us seem to be able to lift this two-kilo weight off our table with our minds," he said as he pointed to the work he and Tahiri were supposed to be doing.

"Then maybe you're doing something wrong," Tionne replied. Both students turned and focused on the large hunk of metal that Tionne had easily lifted onto their desk. The metal moved a centimeter at most.

Anakin looked around the room. Several of the other students had succeeded in lifting an object with their minds. Across the room were two students who looked like huge black flies. They had each lifted their weight. Now they were happily buzzing. Anakin stared at them. They weren't stronger in the Force than he and Tahiri. He was sure of that. So why couldn't he and Tahiri perform this feat?

"We're not concentrating," Tahiri said, interrupting his thoughts. They tried again, but the metal would not move.

"All of you have different strengths," Tionne said. "You are here to figure out where your strengths lie." In frustration, Anakin squeezed his eyes shut and forced his mind to reach into the object. Be light, he commanded. At the same time, Tahiri was focusing on lifting the object. Anakin opened his eyes just in time to see the metal shoot toward the classroom's ceiling. Wham! It struck with a thud. Both Anakin and Tahiri lost their concentration and barely avoided being hit by the weight on its way back down. It landed on their table. The table broke in two.

"Good," Tionne said, hiding a smile. "You're learning your strengths." The rest of the students began to laugh. Anakin scowled. Tahiri giggled.

"How did we do that?" Tahiri whispered to Anakin when the class had settled back to work. Anakin shrugged.

"Beats me. It's weird, but I was asking the metal to be lighter and when I opened my eyes it was shooting toward the ceiling. What'd you do, Tahiri?"

"I just tried again to lift it," Tahiri said. "Guess we somehow make a good team," she added. She looked at Anakin and said softly, "Okay, Anakin, if you say the raft will be there, then it will be there. And don't think I'm not coming with you. Wild banthas couldn't keep me from sneaking out to the river. After all, I've never been rafting be-fore—except in my dreams. Did you know that?" Tahiri didn't wait for an answer. "There's just one thing I've got to tell you before we go, Anakin: I don't know how to swim."

"I already figured that out," Anakin said with a
frown. "I guess that's one of the reasons we've got
to be aboard that silver raft *together*." Anakin
tried to smile at his friend. But in his heart he
was scared. What if he couldn't save Tahiri when
she fell into the river? What if his dream came
true?

SEVEN

Tahiri tiptoed across the floor of her bedroom. She quietly slipped her orange jumpsuit over her nightgown and moved silently to the door. She pushed gently on it, then poked her head into the hallway. No one was there. She crept down the hall. Her bare feet padded softly on the smooth stones. When she reached Anakin's door she knocked once. Anakin had been waiting for his friend. He pushed his door open and Tahiri quickly went inside.

It was almost midnight. All of the instructors and students at the academy were sound asleep. But Tahiri and Anakin had not been able to sleep. They needed to plan how they were going to sneak out of the academy. Tahiri curled up on the cushion next to Anakin's bed. Anakin sat cross-legged beside her.

"What if we both pretend that we're sick," Tahiri suggested to her friend.

Anakin made a face. "Both of us? They'll never believe we're both sick," he said.

"Why not?" Tahiri asked.

"Well, first of all my uncle Luke knows that I've rarely been sick in my life. If I pretended to be sick he'd be really worried. He'd probably call my parents and send me home." He frowned.

"Maybe we should just sneak out at night," he said. "After all, everybody is asleep."

Tahiri shook her head. "It won't work," she said.

"Why not? We'd have hours to explore," Anakin said.

"Because in the dream it's daytime," Tahiri explained. "We have to do exactly what we do in the dream, otherwise we're not following our destiny."

"Tahiri, I don't think we should blindly follow what you believe is our destiny," Anakin replied. "Following our destiny is a pretty romantic notion. It's important, but we have to take other things into consideration."

"Like what?" Tahiri demanded. "Are you talking about that strange voice again?"

"Yes and no," Anakin began. "I think you're right that we are in some way meant to take the silver raft of our dream down the river of Yavin 4. And I think we're meant to do it together. But not just because we've had the same dream. I think there is a lot more involved. And yes, I do mean the voice inside my head. It's real, Tahiri," Anakin said softly. "It's real, and it's not just any voice. I'm just about certain that it's the voice of a Jedi Master."

"How do you know that?" Tahiri cried in surprise.

"I just do," Anakin said. "And the voice leads me to believe that we are both needed somewhere. I don't know where, or why, but it is the voice that I'm following, not just the call of destiny."

"So where does that leave us?" Tahiri asked. "Are we going to raft the river at night?"

"No, I think you're right about going in the daytime, for two reasons. First, it is light in our dream, and that fact may be important. But second, and more important, we should go during the day simply because we don't know where we're going or what we're looking for. Whatever it is we are being drawn to will be easier to see in the light."

"So will we," Tahiri said slowly. "I know that you don't want to think about this, Anakin, but there's a good chance that we are going to get caught. We might even get sent home."

Anakin frowned. He knew that Tahiri was right. "I guess we should just figure out how to sneak away from the academy. And after we raft the river we'll try to get back without anyone seeing us. But we shouldn't count on it," Anakin finally said.

"So how do we sneak out?" Tahiri asked her friend.

Sneaking out of the academy was going to be hard. The instructors would be able to sense their emotions. They would have to be very careful to hide their excitement. It took several hours before Anakin and Tahiri came up with a good idea.

Each afternoon the students were given two hours of free time before dinner. The friends decided that they would leave the academy during this period. The only problem was that two hours wasn't a lot of time. Especially since Anakin and Tahiri didn't know exactly where they were going. But it would have to do. More and more, Anakin felt certain that he and Tahiri were being called to the river for a reason—and that it was a matter of grave importance.

"What day do you want to go?" Tahiri asked Anakin.

He sighed before he answered. "I guess tomorrow afternoon. That means you only have to fall into the river one more time in the dream," Anakin said with a small smile. He knew that falling into the river was terrifying for Tahiri. He didn't want to make her do it any more than she had to.

"Where should we meet?" Tahiri asked her friend.

"The hangar bay in the bottom of the Temple. It has an exit door that opens into the jungle," Anakin said.

"How do you know that?" Tahiri asked in surprise.

"It's that voice in my head again," Anakin explained. Tahiri frowned. Anakin didn't say anything, but he knew that she was worried that they were trusting that voice too much. After all, it could be leading them to use the Force for evil. Anakin sighed. There was only one way to find out. "We'll leave after our morning class and go down to the hangar," he said firmly. "Then we'll sneak out of the Great Temple and make our way to the river."

Tahiri nodded in agreement. With luck they could get back to the academy before the bell for the evening meal, she thought. She didn't want to think of what would happen if they didn't return in time.

"I guess we should get some sleep," Anakin said with a yawn. It was almost dawn. In a few more hours the bell for the morning meal would ring.

"It's a good plan," Tahiri said as she stood up from the cushion. Her orange jumpsuit was rumpled. And her long blonde hair had fallen out of her braid. It hung loose around her shoulders. "Hey, Anakin, if we do get caught and get sent back home, can we still be friends?" Tahiri asked.

Anakin smiled at Tahiri. "Sure thing," he replied. But he knew that his home planet was far away from Tatooine. If he and Tahiri were sent home they might never see each other again. Anakin met Tahiri's green eyes with his blue ones. He could see she also knew this might be their last few hours as friends.

"Sweet dreams," Tahiri said before she left Anakin's room.

Anakin fell asleep quickly. And he had the river dream again. Except this time both he and Tahiri were in the raft. Anakin was in the back, paddling hard. Tahiri sat in front, gripping one side of the raft. The water was crashing in waves over the sides. The wind howled and tossed the small raft sideways just as a gigantic wave slammed it. Tahiri was thrown backward. Anakin turned to spot her in the water, and the surprise of what he saw almost made him fall in too.

"Oh no," Anakin moaned when he saw that Artoo-Detoo was now in the raft with him. "I can't be expected to sneak out with that noisy droid," he cried. But even as he searched the water for Tahiri he knew that tomorrow he would bring Artoo with them. If Artoo was in the dream, then he was meant to be a part of the adventure. Anakin knew that, but it didn't mean he had to like it. A soft bell rang in the distance. Anakin realized it was time to wake up and begin the adventure for real. He rolled over and slowly opened his eyes.

EIGHT

"Tahiri, there's been a slight change of plans," Anakin whispered to his friend over breakfast. "We have to take Artoo-Detoo with us."

Tahiri's jaw dropped. "I don't understand. Why should we take Artoo?" Tahiri didn't receive an answer. She studied her friend for a moment before she spoke again. Anakin looked exhausted. Ever since he'd begun to have her dream, tired purple circles started to appear under his eyes. Tahiri, on the other hand, had slept wonderfully the last few nights. She hadn't had the dream once. "Anakin," Tahiri began again, "you've got to be kidding. We can't take that droid. He'll ruin everything. We can't even understand him. And if he fell into the river we'd never be able to get him out," Tahiri added without stopping for a breath.

"He was in my dream last night," Anakin said

softly. "That means that we might need him wherever we're going."

"And we might *not* need him," Tahiri said with a scowl. "I thought we weren't going to follow our dreams without question," she added.

"Better safe than sorry?" Anakin asked his friend.

"That's true," Tahiri sullenly admitted. "Well, how are we going to get him to sneak away with us?"

"Leave that up to me," Anakin said with a little smile.

It was hard to concentrate on schoolwork that morning. Both Anakin and Tahiri kept looking at their wrist-chronometers. They were excited, nervous, and scared. It seemed like years before class was over. When the other students had filed out of the room, Anakin sauntered over to Artoo-Detoo.

"Hey, Artoo, want to show me around the rest of the Great Temple during my free time?" The droid bleeped several times. "I take it that means yes," Anakin muttered. "Good. There's just one thing. We need to develop a way to understand each other. Let's start with one beep for yes and two beeps for no, okay?" Artoo beeped once. "Let's go, buddy," Anakin said with a smile.

Anakin and Artoo headed away from the group down one of the hallways. Tahiri quickly caught up to them. The three rounded a corner and

Anakin checked to make sure no one was behind
them. Once he was sure they were alone he and
Tahiri began to race down the hallway. Artoo
whistled in surprise, then scooted to follow them.
Anakin knew that his uncle Luke had probably
asked the droid to keep an eye on him. He'd
banked on Artoo's following him once he and
Tahiri started running.

Tahiri's bare feet slapped on the stone floor as
they tore down the stairs that led to the hangar
bay. She didn't see Anakin stopped in front of her
until she'd crashed into his back. He didn't have
to warn her to be quiet. She immediately spotted
Luke Skywalker and Tionne. They were walking
down a hallway on a lower level. A door opened to
their left and the two Jedi disappeared inside.
Anakin and Tahiri both sighed in relief and then
began to run again. By the time they reached the
hangar both were out of breath, and Artoo had
stopped beeping.

Anakin and Tahiri opened a large wooden door
and slid into darkness. Artoo followed behind
them. They began running their hands along the
stone walls, seeking the exit door. "I can't find it,"
Tahiri said in a desperate voice. Then a thought
struck her. "Anakin, the lower level of the Temple
is partially underground. How can there be a
door?" Tahiri cried.

"There has to be some kind of exit to the jungle," Anakin whispered in the darkness. "The

voice said so. We must be doing something wrong." Anakin dropped to his knees and began searching the floor of the storage room. There was a chance that they were looking for the door in the wrong place. His fingers ran along the smooth surface. All of a sudden his left thumb caught on something. It was a thick crack. He traced the crack with his fingers. It was in the shape of a large square. "Tahiri, I think I've found it," he called. Tahiri ran over to Anakin and saw the outline of a trapdoor on the floor beneath her.

"How do we open it?" she asked. Artoo began to beep-beep. "Quiet, you silly droid," Tahiri whispered angrily. Artoo kept double-beeping.

"He's saying no," Anakin said under his breath. Anakin looked up and saw the droid standing by a large wooden handle in the wall. "You're trying to tell us that we're doing this all wrong, aren't you," Anakin whispered to the droid. "Give it a try your way, Artoo," he said. The droid reached up and pulled down the handle with his metal arm. Instantly the doorway in the floor opened.

Anakin looked down. A narrow passage of stone blocks led away from the trapdoor. "This must be the way," Anakin said as he slid into the passage. "Come on, you two," he called from the darkness.

"You first," Tahiri said to the droid. Artoo beeped once and moved forward to the trapdoor. He tipped slightly backward, then rolled into the passageway and out of sight. "My turn," Tahiri whispered. Then she, too, dropped out of sight.

A few minutes later, hot, moist air hit the three as they entered the jungles of Yavin 4. "Follow me," Anakin called as he raced toward the river. Artoo beeped several times.

"I think he knows where he's going, buddy," Tahiri said to the droid. They began to follow Anakin. Tahiri had to stop a few times to help Artoo, who kept getting tangled in the blueleaf shrubs. Anakin was already by the long silver raft when Tahiri and Artoo got to the edge of the river.

"Told you the raft would be here," he said with a shy smile. Tahiri hopped in and they lifted Artoo over the rounded sides of the raft, then pushed it off from the bank. Anakin jumped in at the last second.

"Well, at least we're not rafting in a storm like we do in the dream," Anakin said as he began to paddle. Tahiri sat in the front of the raft staring down at the water. This place is amazing, she thought. Enormous Massassi trees hung down over the river, their branches arching. The sunlight danced off the clear green water.

The only thing that keeps this afternoon from being perfect is Artoo, Tahiri thought. Since they had begun rafting he hadn't stopped whistling and beeping. "Can't you make him be quiet?" Tahiri asked Anakin.

"He must have something on his mind, because he hasn't stopped whistling for ten minutes," Anakin replied. "I wish I'd had more time to figure out a way to understand him."

Tahiri turned back to face the droid. She was going to make Artoo be quiet, even if she had to disconnect his speaker. But when Tahiri turned around she couldn't say a word. She was too shocked by what she saw. "Ah, Anakin, I t-t-think we m-might have a problem," Tahiri finally managed to say.

"What's that?" Anakin asked as he paddled.

"I think Artoo has been trying to tell us to look behind the raft," Tahiri replied. Anakin turned quickly. The sky of Yavin 4 had become black. Large purple storm clouds rolled across it. In a flash the sun was covered and Yavin 4 grew cold and dark. The wind rose, tearing over the river.

"What's going on?" Tahiri yelled to Anakin above the roar of the wind.

"I'm not sure, but I think this might be one of the terrible storms Uncle Luke told me about when I got to Yavin 4. He said that every few months strong winds and rains tear across the moon," Anakin told Tahiri. He didn't tell her that his uncle had also said that perhaps the only safe place to be during the storms was the Great Temple.

Tahiri's sea green eyes grew dark, just like the water of the river. She saw the waves begin to form. "This is going to be just like my dream," she said in dread. "Only this time I might really drown."

"Don't think that way, Tahiri," Anakin commanded. "Just hang on. I'll try to paddle us to land." Tahiri gripped the side of the raft. The water was now crashing over them in giant waves. The raft tipped dangerously to one side.

Tahiri's blonde hair whipped around her face. For a moment she couldn't see. Artoo beeped loudly behind her. Then a gigantic wave hit her and she toppled backward. She couldn't see anything as she tumbled. Then she was in the water. It was bitterly cold. Every time she tried to gasp for breath another wave struck her. Tahiri felt herself beginning to drown. Help me, Anakin, she screamed in her mind. But all she could see was water. And all she could hear were her own cries.

NINE

"Grab the paddle, Tahiri!" Anakin screamed above the storm. He could barely see his friend in the tumbling waves. Her orange jumpsuit flashed between the rolls of water. He watched as Tahiri struggled toward him, her arms thrashing wildly.

"I can't reach the paddle!" she cried.

"Try again," Anakin yelled. Tahiri tried, but was once more swept beneath a wave. She was running out of strength. Anakin didn't know what to do. He had power in his arms, but that couldn't help his friend.

"There are all different kinds of power," a strange voice spoke inside Anakin's head.

"What does that mean?" Anakin screamed into the wind. There was no answer. He turned toward Tahiri. "Try again," he called. But this time his voice wasn't a scream—it was a command, a command said with the power of the

Force. Anakin knew that some Jedi Masters could use their voices to control people. Could it be that he also had that ability? He watched as Tahiri thrashed toward the paddle he was holding out to her. She seemed stronger than before, but Anakin wasn't sure how much longer she could hold herself above the water. He closed his eyes and focused on Tahiri's body, just as he had focused on the two-kilogram weight that he and Tahiri had lifted in class. Be light, he commanded. Anakin opened his eyes and saw that Tahiri's head and shoulders were now above the water.

Before another wave could sweep Tahiri away, she grasped the paddle. "Hang on," Anakin instructed. He leaned over to pull his friend toward him. A large wave hit the side of the raft. Anakin lost his balance and began to fall into the river. For a brief flash his eyes met Tahiri's. They were filled with fear. If Anakin fell into the river they might both drown. Anakin knew he wouldn't be able to concentrate on making Tahiri light or giving her strength if he had to focus on keeping himself afloat.

Anakin watched the wild river dance before his eyes. He knew he was about to plunge into the cold water. He could feel his body falling out of the raft. But just as he was about to be caught by a wave he was yanked hard from behind. Artoo had grabbed the back of Anakin's orange jumpsuit with his metal hand and pulled him to safety.

Anakin then grasped one of Tahiri's hands and dragged her into the raft. He turned to Artoo. "Thanks," he said softly. Artoo bleeped.

Anakin grabbed his paddle and began to furiously stroke. Tahiri lay in the bottom of the raft. "Anakin," she said with wonder, "you used the Force to get me to float and to give me the strength I needed to thrash my way to the raft. I was ready to give up, but your voice wouldn't let me." Anakin gave his friend a smile. Then he turned back to the river.

"We're almost at the shore," Anakin said. "Tahiri, we're going to have to jump out of the raft. The river is going too fast. There's no way I can get the raft to stop."

Tahiri sat up. "What about Artoo?" she asked. "He can't leap into the river."

"We'll have to do what we did in class the other day," Anakin said. "After we jump I'll think about him being light, and you try to lift him." There was no time to talk about it. "Okay, it's time," Anakin said as their raft raced by the side of the river. "Jump!"

Both students landed hard on the bank of the river and then rolled to a stop. "Now Artoo," Anakin yelled to Tahiri. The droid was still on the raft. He was being swept quickly down the river. Anakin and Tahiri concentrated. Artoo floated in the air toward them. Suddenly he dropped in the water.

"Oops," Tahiri muttered. Then she closed her eyes and focused. Moments later Artoo landed safely beside the two students. Both Anakin and Tahiri stared down the river as their silver raft continued to race along the waters. "Guess we're not *rafting* back to the academy," Tahiri said under her breath.

It had begun to rain—not just to rain, but to pour. "We've got to find some shelter," Tahiri said to Anakin. The three raced into the jungle in search of a place to hide from the storm. The weather was getting worse. The wind was so strong that it almost carried Tahiri away, and she had to wrap her arms around the trunk of a Massassi tree every time it blew. "There's nowhere to hide!" Tahiri cried.

Anakin grabbed his friend's hand and pulled her deeper into the jungle. They were surrounded by Massassi trees, climbing ferns, and large, deep pink flowers. Jungle animals, their fur blue and gold, raced across the floor of the jungle. They must be the woolamanders that Jacen described to me, Anakin thought. But they usually lived in the tops of the Massassi trees, he remembered. Anakin guessed that the storm had brought the animals to the ground, that the woolamanders were looking for a safe place to hide too.

"Are those animals dangerous?" Tahiri asked her friend as they ran through the jungle.

"I think they're called woolamanders, and if I

remember right my brother said that they only eat plants," Anakin shouted. They saw hundreds of woolamanders as they ran. Several times the two friends had to stop to wait for Artoo, who kept getting caught on roots and shrubs. Meanwhile the storm was getting worse. If they didn't find shelter soon they would be in real trouble.

"Hey, Tahiri! Look over there," Anakin said. Tahiri saw the outline of a building. They ran through the jungle until they reached it. It looked kind of like the Great Temple, but much smaller. And it was in ruins. "I think this is one of the structures that was built by the Massassi people," Anakin said.

"Who are they?" Tahiri asked.

"They were a race who used to live on this planet," Anakin explained. "They disappeared thousands of years ago."

"Well, then they won't mind if we go inside," Tahiri giggled.

They ran to the palace. Anakin stopped outside the door to the crumbling building. High above him were dark letters carved into the tan stone. The letters were not Basic. "I wonder what those symbols mean," he said.

"Who cares—let's get inside," Tahiri yelled. Artoo bleeped in agreement, and the three headed through the doorway.

Inside the palace it was dark. Tahiri heard the

clicks of hundreds of scurrying feet. "Anakin, do you hear that?" she whispered.

Anakin pushed his wet hair out of his eyes and tried to see in the darkness. "I hear it, but I can't see anything," he replied. With a beep and a click, Artoo lit up the room with a beam of light.

"I knew there was a reason we brought him along," Tahiri said. They stared around the room. Thousands of tiny black eyes stared back. Woolamanders were everywhere!

"Yes, I'm sure of it—they don't eat people," Anakin said to Tahiri. He had sensed her fear.

"Okay, but I still don't have to like them," Tahiri muttered.

"This must be the Palace of the Woolamander," Anakin said. "It was named years ago by some guy who was exploring the planet. The woolamanders must have been here then too."

"As long as we're here, let's explore," Tahiri suggested.

Why not, Anakin thought. It had been a long time since they'd snuck out of the academy. Heck, Luke Skywalker was probably thinking up some kind of punishment, or maybe even getting the shuttle ready to take them home. It couldn't hurt to do a little bit of exploring.

TEN

Anakin and Tahiri walked through a large stone hallway in the Palace of the Woolamander. Anakin noticed that the same letters he'd seen carved above the door were repeated on the stone walls inside the palace. Tahiri interrupted his thoughts.

"So what happened to the Massassi?" she asked.

"Nobody really knows," Anakin replied as he ran his hands along the palace walls. "But there was one story about them that my father once told me," he said. Anakin's voice echoed in the empty hallways as he began to tell Tahiri the story.

"Years ago there was a man named Dr'uun Unnh. He was from the star system Sullust. Dr'uun Unnh was a Sullustan. Have you ever seen one?" Anakin asked Tahiri. She shook her

69

head. "Well, Sullustans are humanoids with round ears, large round eyes, and heavy cheeks that hang down their faces. Anyway, Dr'uun Unnh was a history and nature lover, and he spent a lot of his life studying Yavin 4. He studied all of the old temples on this planet. By digging beneath the temples he learned about the Massassi.

"According to Dr'uun," Anakin continued, "over five thousand years ago the exiled Sith magicians —whom nobody knows much about except that they're feared and that Darth Vader was one— settled on Yavin 4. The magicians married the natives to create the race of Massassi. A thousand years later an evil Jedi Knight named Exar Kun came to Yavin 4 to enslave the Massassi, build more temples, and resurrect the Sith teachings. Exar Kun was wiped out in the Great Sith War, which pitted the Old Republic and the Jedi Knights against the followers of Kun, who called himself the Dark Lord of the Sith."

"That story gives me the chills," Tahiri said. "Especially the part about Darth Vader being part of the Sith."

"Yeah, me too," Anakin agreed.

Tahiri and Anakin could still hear the storm raging outside the palace walls. They turned a corner and stood before a crumbling wall of stone blocks. "I guess this is a dead end," Anakin said. They were just about to turn around when Artoo's light stopped at a hole in the wall. Tahiri walked forward and peered through the hole. She could see a long stone stairway that wound down through the floor of the palace. Before Anakin could stop her Tahiri had crawled through the hole. "Wait, Tahiri," Anakin called. "Someone built this wall so that we wouldn't go down those stairs," he said.

"Well, the wall is crumbling, so maybe now we're meant to go down," Tahiri called back.

Artoo began to beep and blip loudly. "I don't think he wants us to go down there," Anakin said. "And he's not the only one." Anakin had poked his head through the hole and could actually sense something evil floating up the stone stairs. The hairs on his arms rose. Artoo continued to beep-beep. Anakin crawled through the hole and joined his friend.

Tahiri hadn't started down the stone stairway. "There's something evil here," she whispered in a small voice. "Anakin, what if those Dark Lord guys are still here?"

"Maybe we should turn back," Anakin whispered.

"No," Tahiri said fiercely, her green eyes flashing. "We've come this far. I'm not going to turn back just because I sense that something bad is trying to scare us away. Anakin, you said that you felt like we were being called to perform an important task, maybe it's something that will help us become Jedi Knights. If that's true, there's no way I'm going to turn back." Tahiri began to make her way down the stairway. There were loose stones and several times she almost fell.

"Tahiri, wait," Anakin called, but she kept moving. Anakin rushed down after his friend.

This is not the way I like to do things, Anakin thought. I like to think, to figure out the choices. He slid his feet along the broken stairs. He thought about the fact that Darth Vader had been a part of the Sith. He always tried not to think of Vader as his grandfather. But Vader had once been Anakin Skywalker, Luke and Leia's father. And that made him Anakin's grandfather. But that was before he began using the Force for evil and became Vader.

Anakin wished his parents hadn't named him after his mom's father. He had once asked his mother why she had chosen to name him after Vader. "You weren't named after Darth Vader," Leia had explained. "You were named after my father. He was Anakin Skywalker, not Vader. And before he died your grandfather did turn away from the dark side. He died saving your uncle Luke's life." Leia had told Anakin that it was important to remember that the power of the Force could turn even a good man to the dark side. "Anakin, to me your name reminds me of hope," Leia had explained. "Hope that even when a Jedi uses the Force for the dark side he can choose to turn back to the light. Just as my father Anakin Skywalker did."

Right now Anakin didn't need any reminders about the dark side—it was all around him. It coated the walls of the stairway in sticky darkness. Anakin could feel it trying to cover him. It tugged at the sleeves of his jumpsuit and swirled around his head. He pushed it aside with his mind and followed his friend down the spiral stairway. Whatever was down there, he and Tahiri would meet it together.

"I am going to get kicked out of the Jedi academy for this," Anakin said under his breath as he climbed down the stairway. "Not only that, I'm probably going to run into that Dark Lord of the Sith and end up in even bigger trouble."

Anakin could hardly see Tahiri's back in the darkness as the two climbed down the stairs. And he could barely hear Artoo beeping in the distance. The stairway was too broken and winding for the droid to manage, so Artoo had stayed behind. Anakin was sure that the droid was telling them both to come back.

"Tahiri, will you please wait for me? I can't see anything," Anakin called out. Without Artoo's light, which had been lost right after the stairway turned away from the crumbling wall, it was almost impossible to see. At least if Tahiri was right in front of him, he said to himself, he would be able to tell where to walk.

"I can't see any better than you can," Tahiri called back. "This is quite an adventure, isn't it, Anakin," she began to chatter. "We'd probably just be looking at holographs if we were back at the Temple right now. Instead we're—yipes!"

Anakin had heard his friend begin to fall before she'd cried out, and now there was a quiet rumble as the stone she was on gave way. "Tahiri, are you okay?" he called as he tried to move quickly down the stairs. He could barely see her when he bent down.

"Yeah, I think so," she said. "Serves me right for talking so much instead of concentrating on where I was going."

Anakin smiled in the darkness. He moved to help Tahiri to her feet. She gave a small yelp. "What's wrong?" he asked.

"My foot is caught under something," Tahiri explained.

Anakin searched the darkness around Tahiri's foot with his hand. "Your foot is wedged under a heavy stone," Anakin groaned as he tried to move the rock.

"Let's do this together," Tahiri suggested. They concentrated on using the Force. Slowly the stone rose and then fell to one side. Tahiri pulled her foot out of a small hole.

"Is it broken or cut?" Anakin asked.

Tahiri bent down to feel her bare foot. "Not a scratch," she said in amazement. A moment later her hand brushed against something. Something that was not another rock.

ELEVEN

"What is this?" Tahiri muttered as she lifted up the object by her foot. She ran her hands over the thing. It was strangely smooth and thin.

"Let me feel it," Anakin said. Tahiri handed it to him. He ran his fingers along it until he reached what felt like two wide bumps. There were four thin, short objects coming out of the bumps. Each of them was about five centimeters long. They were all bent in several places. Anakin closed his eyes. He knew what this was. "Let's keep going," he said in a weak voice.

"What is it, Anakin?" Tahiri asked. She could tell her friend knew exactly what the object was.

"You don't want to know," Anakin told her.

"Yes I do," she replied stubbornly.

"All right. I'm pretty sure that it's an old bone."

"A bone from what?" Tahiri asked.

"I think it's the arm and hand bone of one of the

ancient Massassi," Anakin explained. "What's more, I think it was a child's." Tahiri was silent. "Do you want to turn back?" Anakin gently asked his friend.

"No," Tahiri replied. "We have to go on."

"Okay. But since you won't turn back, at least let's do this together," Anakin said. They joined hands and slowly walked downward.

The stone staircase was much longer than Anakin had imagined. It wound in a tight spiral deep into the surface of the planet. At certain spots the stairway was so narrow that Anakin could touch the stone walls on both sides of it. The walls felt sticky.

"We must be hundreds of meters down," Tahiri said. "Why would someone build such a big staircase and then block it with a stone wall?" she asked out loud. "Somebody must have wanted to keep wherever we're going a big secret," Tahiri answered herself breathlessly. A moment later she stubbed her toe. "Ouch, I wish we had a glowrod," she grumbled.

"We won't need one in a few minutes," Anakin replied.

"How do you know that?" Tahiri asked.

"I just have a feeling," Anakin said slowly. The two tightened their grip on each other's hand.

The stairway circled ten more times. But just as Anakin had said, light began to appear. But the light was not like the light from Artoo. It was a dusting of glittering gold that appeared in spots on the stairway and the stone walls. The gold glowed in the dark. Tahiri touched one of the spots and her finger began to tingle. Moments later they heard the voices.

"Go back," came the rumbling moans. "Go back or fear for your lives," the voices called. Anakin could almost hear his own heart pounding. "We are the followers of the ancient Sith teachings. We are sworn to protect this place from intruders. Go back or die!"

Tahiri stopped, her hand clenching his tightly. "Did you hear that?" she whispered.

"Yeah," Anakin said shakily.

"Maybe we should get out of here," Tahiri suggested. Anakin wanted nothing more than to agree. He desperately wanted to race up the stairs and back into the light. He was terrified that he was being drawn to the dark side of the Force, that something was trying to turn him toward evil. But Anakin couldn't turn back. He knew in his heart that there was a reason that he and Tahiri were here. He also knew they might never get another chance to find out that reason, that it would be impossible if they were kicked out of the academy and returned to their home planets.

"Tahiri, you go back if you want," Anakin whispered. "I have to go forward. I don't know why, but I know that the voice I heard in my head was not something evil calling me."

"This is a dark place. You are not welcome here. Only those that serve the dark side of the Force can stay," the evil followers of the Sith teachings rumbled.

Tahiri began to shake. She hated being afraid almost as much as she hated being told what to do. Anakin squeezed her hand tightly, and Tahiri stopped shaking. "Anakin, I won't go back. We're a team," Tahiri said in a tiny voice. "Anyway, if those voices could really hurt us, they'd be doing just that. Right, Anakin?" she asked. Anakin didn't answer.

The two friends moved forward. The evil voices began whispering their threats. "Go back . . . go back . . . or strike at us to kill us."

"Quit it!" Tahiri finally screamed. She'd had enough of the voices. "We don't want to listen to you anymore!" she shouted into the darkness. "And we won't use the Force for evil. We believe in using the Force for peace, knowledge, and defense, not to attack. So just be quiet." The voices stopped.

"And Anakin," Tahiri said in exasperation as she turned to face her friend. "Stop thinking that you are the only one that beings who serve the dark side of the Force are interested in. I'm hearing those voices too. Just because your grandfather was Darth Vader doesn't mean you are going to serve the dark side of the Force. You aren't your grandfather. You are your own person, and you can make your own choices."

Anakin was speechless. He thought he had kept his feelings private; he hadn't known that Tahiri understood about his grandfather. But he did know that some of what Tahiri had just said was true. He wasn't Anakin Skywalker. He was Anakin Solo, the son of Han and Leia. Still, he couldn't help wondering if there was something evil planted within him. Something that would make him use his powers to serve the dark side of the Force. After all, he was directly related to Darth Vader.

"I don't know if yelling at those voices was a good thing or a bad thing," Anakin finally said.

"At least whatever it was has shut up," Tahiri grumbled. Anakin grabbed his friend's hand and gave it a gentle squeeze. They circled down again, and suddenly Anakin and Tahiri found themselves on the last step of the stairway. They had finally reached the bottom. Before them was a small stone room that glowed with golden light.

There were patches of golden glitter everywhere. They seemed to be seeping from the wall at the far end of the room. Anakin moved to the wall and gently touched the stones with his fingers, which soon began to tingle. "The gold is coming from behind this wall, Tahiri," Anakin whispered. "There must be a hidden room back there." But how were they going to move thousands of kilos of stone? Anakin wondered. Sure they had lifted Artoo, and even a two-kilo hunk of metal, but this was different.

As if reading his mind, Tahiri said softly, "I guess we should give it a try."

Sweat dripped down Anakin's forehead. He had been trying to move the stone blocks for a long time. Tahiri rubbed her fingers against her eyes. The strain of trying to move the stones had given her a terrible headache. Neither of the two Jedi students had been able to move the blocks even a centimeter. They walked over to the last step of the stairway and sat down. "I don't want to give up," Tahiri began, "but this just isn't working."

Anakin nodded at his friend's words. There has to be another way, he thought; maybe strength isn't the answer. Then he heard the voice in his head again. He turned to Tahiri, his blue eyes open wide. "The voice in my head just spoke again," he said softly. "It said that there are different kinds of strength. One is physical, like the lifting of the droid. Another is the strength of the mind." Tahiri stared at her friend. For once she was speechless.

Anakin thought about those words. He and Tahiri had proven that they could move heavy objects. But their use of the Force was still limited; they were not powerful Jedi yet. What exactly was "the strength of the mind." What had the voice in his head meant? He remembered a gift his father had once given him. It was a laser puzzle, the kind that had thousands of smaller puzzles within it. His father had said it would take his strength to figure them out. But it hadn't taken any muscle for Anakin to solve the puzzle. He had used his mind, not his body.

"That's it, Tahiri!" Anakin cried. "The stone blocks are a puzzle that we have to figure out with the strength of our minds. We solve the puzzle, and we'll find out what's behind that wall!"

TWELVE

"I've never been very good at puzzles," Tahiri said to Anakin.

"It's not that hard. You just have to look for patterns," Anakin explained. "Try to look at the shapes of the stones or the cracks between them. Maybe you'll see something in them," Anakin offered. Together he and Tahiri walked along the stone wall.

"All I see is a lot of gold glitter," Tahiri grumbled. She still had a splitting headache.

"Hey, this looks like an arrow," Tahiri said, pointing to a crack in one of the stones. It was a dark brown, and wiggled in a curving line up the stone wall. "There's another one," she cried. Anakin stood beside his friend.

"You're right—there are at least five arrows that I can see from here. And they all seem to be pointing up," Anakin noted.

"Well, then that's where I'm going," Tahiri said with a grin. She began to climb the stone wall. Her small feet wedged carefully between the stones and her hands gripped tiny bumps on the rock.

"Tahiri, be careful," Anakin called to his friend. Tahiri had climbed halfway up the strange stone wall and now stood two meters off the ground.

"There's got to be some sort of secret button that will open this wall," Tahiri said. Her hands flew around the corners of the stone blocks. She didn't feel anything, so she moved higher. Tahiri was still following the brown arrows. Only now the arrows had grown larger and were much easier to see.

"It can't be this simple," Anakin called to his friend. "If the secret to opening the wall was arrows and a hidden button then anyone could find it. This wall has been standing for thousands of years. The secret just can't be that easy."

"Maybe we're really smart," Tahiri called down to her friend.

"Tahiri, you should come back down," Anakin instructed. "We need to think this through. Those voices that told us to go back or fear for our lives? Maybe they meant that if we do something wrong down here we could be in danger. Anyway, we aren't using the strength of our minds to figure out the puzzle. You're just using the strength of your muscles."

Tahiri grunted in response. She was almost to the top of the wall. Her hands ran along a stone block. There was something there. It felt like a smooth button. "Anakin! I think I've found the secret button!" she called.

Anakin was overcome by an immediate sense of dread, so strong that he could almost taste it. "Don't do anything!" Anakin screamed to his friend. But it was too late.

Tahiri pushed the smooth button. It made a soft popping sound, but nothing happened. Tahiri pushed the button again, this time harder. A loud rumbling began. "Hey, it worked!" Tahiri called down. "Do you hear that, Anakin? Something is happening. Maybe a hidden door is about to open," Tahiri suggested breathlessly.

Anakin's neck was bent back so far that he felt it might break. He stood staring up at his friend. When he heard the rumbling sound he knew something wasn't right. No doorway was opening. Anakin looked above Tahiri's head. A big block of stone had come loose. If his friend didn't move quickly the stone would drop from the roof and crush her!

There was no time to shout a warning. Anakin closed his eyes and concentrated on pushing the stone to the side. A thunderous crash jolted Anakin's eyes open. He turned to see that the stone block had landed centimeters from his left foot. It had missed them both. Tahiri was scrambling down the wall toward him.

"Anakin, that rock would have crushed me if you hadn't moved it!" Tahiri cried.

"We had better think things through before we push any more secret buttons," Anakin said gruffly. Tahiri nodded. "Okay, so now we know that there are traps built into the wall," Anakin said.

"And we know that a wrong move could hurt us," Tahiri added. "We also know that it is impossible to move the biggest stones with our minds. The only thing I've been able to move is all this glittery gold stuff," Tahiri said as she brushed off her jumpsuit. It was covered in golden dust.

"You look like a magic fairy," Anakin laughed. Even Tahiri's eyelashes were glittering with dust.

"Watch it or I'll cover you with this stuff," Tahiri giggled back. Just to prove her point, she ran her hands along the wall to pick up glitter and then shook them over Anakin's head. His hair sparkled.

"Very funny," Anakin said as he tried to shake the glitter off. "Hey, Tahiri, what if this glittery gold stuff really is magic?" Anakin asked.

Tahiri made a face at her friend. "Next thing you're going to say is that the glitter is the way we will unlock the wall," she added with a laugh.

"I think it is, Tahiri. This golden stuff is the only thing we've been able to move. Let's try rubbing it along the stones to see if we can highlight any cracks or pathways that we haven't seen."

"It's worth a try," Tahiri agreed.

Anakin moved to the far left wall and began to rub the golden glitter along the stones. In most spots it rained down to the floor and formed piles of gold. Tahiri had begun to rub the glitter along the same wall from the other end. "It's not showing us anything," she grumbled.

"Keep trying," Anakin said. As he reached the center of the wall, Anakin began to notice that a thin line of gold was sticking to some of the stones. He bent down and continued to rub the glitter on them. Tahiri had almost reached the spot where he was rubbing. She crouched by the bottom stone.

"So the glitter sticks in some spots," Tahiri began. "But I don't see a doorway."

Anakin moved back and looked at the lines where the golden dust had stuck. "Tahiri," he said in an awed voice, "step back and look." Tahiri moved away from the wall.

"Holy bantha!" she cried. "Anakin, it's the outline of a child!" Anakin nodded at his friend. Before them a single golden line traced the form of a child on the stone wall. Tahiri raced forward and tried to push the outline in. The stone wall didn't move. "How do we open it?" Tahiri asked in a desperate voice.

"Look, Tahiri," Anakin replied. "To the right of

the figure is another outline—it looks like a hand-print, doesn't it? Maybe that's what triggers the secret door." Tahiri moved to the golden hand and gently placed her own palm over the print. Nothing happened.

"You try, Anakin," Tahiri whispered. Anakin stepped forward and placed his palm on the golden print. Again nothing happened. "What do we do now?" Tahiri asked her friend. "We seemed so close to unlocking the wall. . . ." Tahiri's voice trailed off as she watched her friend race toward the stone stairway. "Where are you going?" Tahiri cried.

"I'll be right back," Anakin called. Moments later Anakin returned to the room with the small bone Tahiri had discovered on the stairway. "Maybe our hands aren't exactly the right shape," Anakin offered in a breathless voice. Tahiri nodded in excitement.

Anakin walked toward the golden figure, the Massassi child's hand stretched out before him. He placed the skeletal fingers against the wall, and they clicked dully against the stones. Then, as the fingertips of the bony hand touched the golden print, they began to disappear. Anakin kept pushing until the entire hand had vanished inside the wall.

"It fits," Tahiri yelled. With a loud click and a gentle hiss of air, the door swung open. A golden light flooded the room. It was much brighter than the glitter. Anakin and Tahiri moved forward, holding hands as they walked inside the secret room.

THIRTEEN

A gigantic crystal globe was in the center of the chamber. It reached to the ceiling and was almost as wide as the whole room. The globe was filled with swirls of golden glitter. It looks like a sparkling dust storm on Tatooine, Tahiri thought. She moved to touch the globe. Before Anakin could warn her to be careful she was tossed back into the stone wall. Anakin raced over to his friend.

"I'm okay," she said as she rose to her feet. "Guess there's some kind of force field around that thing. Oh no, what's this creature?" Tahiri cried, jumping backward.

Anakin peered over to the spot where his friend had fallen. Curled up at the base of a stone block was a small creature. He hadn't seen it at first because its fur was the exact brown and golden color of the stone wall. It seemed to be sleeping. Its closed eyes were large and so round that the lids stuck out several centimeters. The creature's body was about one meter long and its floppy ears draped down to the stone floor. Anakin bent to touch the being's fur. It stuck straight out but was surprisingly soft.

"Anakin, I think it's waking up," Tahiri warned. Anakin backed away. The creature opened one large eye, which was at once a swirl of brown, green, and blue. It studied the two friends. "Do you think it's dangerous?" Tahiri whispered. Anakin shrugged. He wasn't sure. Then the being stretched and yawned.

"He doesn't seem too worried about us," Anakin said.

"Ikrit, Ikrit, Ikrit!" the creature sat up and whistled in a high-pitched voice. Anakin raised his eyebrows questioningly. "Ikrit, Ikrit, Ikrit!" the creature whistled again. Then it curled up its small hands and pounded its chest. "Ikrit, Ikrit, Ikrit!"

"I think it's trying to tell us its name is Ikrit," Tahiri said with a giggle. "Okay, so your name is Ikrit. Pleased to meet you. I'm Tahiri and this is Anakin Solo," she said in a polite voice. It was really kind of cute, she thought. Ikrit stared right at her with its large round eyes. Now they were pure green, just like her own. For a second she could have sworn it winked at her!

Then Ikrit rose and scurried on all fours around the golden globe. It looked like it was checking to make sure the globe was all right. It sat down in front of Anakin when it was done. Then its fur changed color. It was now frost white.

Anakin turned back to the globe. What was it? And why did he feel so sad when he looked at it? Anakin closed his eyes and tried to use the Force to understand the golden globe. For a moment he thought he heard whispers. His eyes flew open. Maybe he and Tahiri were not alone. But no one else was in the room except the creature Ikrit. Anakin closed his eyes again. This time he was sure he heard whispers. The whispers and cries of children. He turned to Tahiri to tell her. She looked frightened.

"Anakin, I know this is going to sound crazy," Tahiri whispered, "but I think I saw a hand pressed against the inside of the globe." Anakin turned back to the globe and peered into the golden light. He could not see anything. "And that's not all I have to tell you," Tahiri said in a small voice. Anakin turned to face his friend. "The hand was a child's."

Anakin whirled back to the globe. He still couldn't see anything. "Tahiri, I can't see anything, but I believe you. Something is inside that globe. When I close my eyes and reach out to it with the Force I can hear children whispering and crying," Anakin said.

Tahiri looked at her friend in horror. She wanted to break the globe open and free whoever was inside of it. But neither of them could touch the globe without being thrown back by its powerful force field.

Ikrit began to leap and jump in the air. "What's it doing?" Tahiri asked.

"I think it's just playing," Anakin said. Ikrit leapt onto Anakin's shoulder and covered the boy's eyes. "Hey, quit it," he said. But Ikrit wouldn't get down from his shoulders. It yanked at Anakin's hair and tweaked his nose. Anakin reached up to pull the creature down. His wrist-chronometer flashed in the golden light. Ikrit turned Anakin's wrist so that he could play with the instrument.

"He must like how it flashes in the light," Tahiri said.

"Oh, my gosh!" Anakin cried when he saw the time flashing. "We've been here for six hours! Everyone at the academy must be out looking for us. We've got to get out of here. If they find us in this secret room, everything will be lost."

"What will be lost?" Tahiri asked. "And how do you know?"

"It's just a feeling, a terrible feeling that if we are discovered here we will fail in whatever we are meant to do. And we will fail more beings than just ourselves," Anakin replied. "It's that feeling of dread, and the voice inside my head."

"What does the voice say?" Tahiri questioned.

"It says get out of here now!" Anakin cried. The

two friends raced out of the room, with Ikrit at their heels.

Tahiri and Anakin charged up the stone stairway. It was easier this time; they were covered with enough golden glitter to light their way. Ikrit followed behind them, and every few minutes he whistled, "Ikrit, Ikrit, Ikrit."

"We know your name already," Anakin grumbled at the creature. Its large eyes, now the same ice blue as Anakin's, stared at the boy.

"Ikrit, Ikrit, Ikrit," it whistled again. But this time Anakin felt like the creature was laughing at him.

On their way up the stairs Tahiri stopped to replace the old bone she had found. She held it up. Its shiny white surface was lit by golden light. It's almost beautiful in a sad way, Tahiri thought. Anakin put his hand on her shoulder. "We've got to get out of here," he said softly. Tahiri put the bone down gently, and they began to once again race up the stairs.

It hadn't seemed such a long way down, Anakin thought as he struggled to catch his breath. The creature Ikrit didn't even look winded. Strange, Anakin thought. That thing had been locked up inside the room with the golden globe. Who knows how long Ikrit had been sleeping there—a year? A thousand years? Had it eaten in all that time? Now it was racing up the steps with them. And it didn't even look tired!

Anakin heard Artoo-Detoo bleeping before he saw him through the hole in the wall. He wondered if the droid had been calling to them the whole time. For a moment he felt guilty. After all, it was Artoo who had saved them from drowning in the river. And it was Artoo who had discovered the hole in the wall. Maybe I've been too hard on the droid, Anakin thought.

As Anakin climbed through the hole he softly whispered an apology to the droid. For a moment Artoo was silent. But when the droid saw Ikrit bounce through the wall he immediately began his beeping and blipping. "Ikrit, Ikrit, Ikrit," the creature whistled. Ikrit jumped onto the rounded top of the droid. Artoo whirled in circles, trying to throw Ikrit off. But Ikrit remained calmly seated on the droid.

Tahiri, Anakin, and Artoo, with Ikrit still sitting on Artoo's head, raced toward the front hallway of the palace. Anakin heaved open the door and they stepped out into the jungle. It was still raining softly. But the storm had ended. The winds had stopped tearing through the jungle, and the night sky was almost clear enough to allow the stars to be seen. Anakin turned to have one last look at the Palace of the Woolamander. He stared at the dark letters carved above the doorway. "I wish I knew what those letters meant," Anakin whispered to himself. Maybe, he thought, they had something to do with the golden globe.

"Stop staring at those symbols," Tahiri said to her friend as she tugged on his arm. "We will never have the chance to find out what they mean if we don't get back to the academy."

"What's the rush," Anakin said. "Chances are pretty good that they're going to be really upset we've been gone so long."

Tahiri scowled at her friend. "We should at least try," she scolded.

FOURTEEN

Quickly Anakin, Tahiri, Artoo, and Ikrit walked back into the jungle. The rain had soon soaked them. Puddles of glittering gold water pooled at Anakin's and Tahiri's feet. The rain was washing all the gold off their hair and jumpsuits. Neither of the friends noticed. It was dark, and they wondered if they would be able to find their way back to the Great Temple through the jungle now that they had lost their raft.

"Ikrit, Ikrit, Ikrit" the strange white creature whistled. Anakin turned and saw that Artoo was stuck in a large hole.

"Must be a runyip hole," Anakin grumbled as he and Tahiri struggled to lift the droid.

"What are runyips?" Tahiri asked as she pushed a wet strand of blonde hair from her face.

"My brother Jacen told me about them. They're jungle animals," Anakin explained. "They have

101

claws on their toes that they use to dig for food. A runyip must have dug this large hole to hide from the storm." At that very moment a shaggy creature with brown and green fur stuck its long nose out of the hole. Artoo bleeped in surprise. Tahiri leapt backward. "They only eat plants," Anakin laughed. The runyip popped out of the hole and darted into the jungle. Anakin watched its white-spotted tail bounce into the distance. Then he turned back to the droid and helped lift him out of the hole.

"Which way should we go?" Anakin asked his friend. Tahiri shook her head. "Well, I guess we should head this way," Anakin said as he pointed into the jungle. "I'm not sure it's the right way back to the academy, but it's better than just standing here."

"Ikrit, Ikrit, Ikrit," the furry animal on Artoo's head whistled.

"That's a lot of help," Tahiri muttered.

Artoo began to beep-beep repeatedly. Then he rolled away from the group. "Artoo is saying no," Anakin said as he stopped in his tracks. "We must be heading the wrong way—let's follow the droid." Tahiri nodded.

Tahiri and Anakin began to follow Artoo. For several minutes Tahiri was silent. This was a rare occurrence, but Tahiri was thinking. How were they going to persuade Luke Skywalker not to kick them out of the academy? They had broken one of Luke's rules. Tahiri wondered if she should take the blame for Anakin. She couldn't stand the idea that he might get kicked out. It was vitally important for him to become a Jedi. Anakin's whole family was strong in the Force. He was meant to be a Jedi. If he was returned home he would be so ashamed, she said to herself. And worst of all, he would never have the chance to complete the important task that had drawn both of them to raft the river of Yavin 4.

If Tahiri was sent back to Tatooine no one would really care, she reflected sadly. The Sand People would just take her back. It didn't matter to them whether she was a Jedi or not. They only cared about searching for water and other treasures. She was just another worker to them. That thought made Tahiri a little sad. She wished that she had a family. People that worried about her. People who cared what happened to her.

"Anakin," Tahiri began in a firm voice. "I'm going to take the blame for you."

Anakin stopped in his tracks and stared at his friend. "How can you even think I'd let you do that, Tahiri?"

"Listen to me," Tahiri said, staring up into Anakin's eyes. "I don't have any family. No one cares if I get sent back home. But there are a lot of people counting on you to be a great Jedi Knight like your uncle. Don't you see, I didn't even know what a Jedi was a few weeks ago. It doesn't matter if I'm returned to Tatooine. I don't have a destiny to fulfill."

"What you're saying isn't true," Anakin interrupted her. "It's true that I would be ashamed if I was sent back home, but we don't know for sure that that will happen. I believe in my heart that I'm meant to be a Jedi Knight. But so are you. Tionne and Uncle Luke wouldn't have brought you to Yavin 4 if you weren't strong in the Force. And even if you aren't that important to the Sand People, you're important to me. *I'm* your family now. I care about what happens to you. And there is no way I would let you take the blame for what we did together. We're a team."

Tahiri smiled. Then the two friends turned to follow Artoo through the jungle. Neither knew at that moment for sure whether they were headed toward or away from the academy. Giant Massassi trees surrounded them. They could see woolamanders and runyips darting through the jungle. They were unsure if they were lost, but Artoo kept rolling forward, Ikrit still perched on his dome. "He seems to know where he's going," Tahiri said.

Anakin shrugged. He hoped Tahiri was right. They had been walking in the jungle for an hour. It was past midnight.

"We just *can't* get kicked out of the academy," Tahiri said to her friend as they walked beneath the giant Massassi trees. "If that happens we will

never get to return to the palace. And we'll never
learn about the golden globe. Something is very
wrong inside that globe, Anakin," Tahiri said
softly. "And we've got to figure out what it is."
Anakin was quiet. "I don't mean to interrupt your
thoughts, Anakin," Tahiri said a bit sarcastically,
"but just in case we are actually close to the academy, I think we should figure out just what we
are going to tell your Uncle Luke."

"If we tell him the truth, we'll be in big trouble," Anakin said.

"Those aren't the same words you used in the
palace," Tahiri countered thoughtfully. "When I
asked you what would happen if we were discovered near the golden globe, you said that a feeling
of dread and the voice inside your head had told
you that 'everything will be lost.' What exactly
does that mean?" Tahiri asked.

"I think it means that we have to keep the
golden globe a secret or whatever we saw inside of
it will be destroyed," Anakin explained.

"Okay, let's tell Luke that we went for a walk
and got lost," Tahiri suggested. It wasn't a great
excuse, but it was true—they had gotten lost trying to return to the Great Temple. In the end,
they'd still broken one of Luke's rules, but it
wouldn't be as bad as telling him they'd gone into
an old palace. The old palaces were falling apart;
Luke would be angry that she and Anakin had
gone into one. And he might also ask what was

inside the palace. Given Anakin's strong feelings and the voice in his head, it didn't seem wise to tell Luke everything they had seen.

Anakin agreed they should use Tahiri's excuse. It was the only way to follow the warnings in his head and heart without directly lying. But Anakin knew that if Luke asked him for the whole truth, he would have to give it—regardless of the outcome. He simply couldn't lie to his uncle.

The group reached a narrow wooden bridge that crossed the river. On the other side loomed the Great Temple. "Wish I'd known about this bridge before I got into that raft and almost drowned," Tahiri grumbled. "Either way, I guess we're home," she said in a soft, scared voice. Slowly Tahiri, Anakin, and Artoo crossed the bridge. Ikrit had disappeared.

"Look who is waiting by the door," Anakin warned.

FIFTEEN

Luke Skywalker's black jumpsuit had faded into the night, but his face was easy to see. It was a tired and unhappy face. And it wore a scowl. Anakin, Tahiri, and Artoo moved toward the Jedi Knight.

"Where have you been?" Luke Skywalker asked Anakin and Tahiri in a stern voice. He had been waiting on the front steps of the Great Temple for his students to return. "We have been searching the academy and the jungle for both of you. You are in deep trouble." Anakin bowed his head. He was afraid that he was about to be kicked out of the academy for breaking one of Luke's rules. If that happened, he knew, he and Tahiri would never be able to return to the golden globe.

"We went for a walk and then the storm came up and we got lost." Anakin heard Tahiri say.

"You got lost?" Luke repeated in disbelief. Artoo

107

beeped softly. Luke stared at the droid. "Artoo, you're telling me that you had to guide these students back to the academy?" Anakin and Tahiri looked at each other in surprise. Artoo was helping them!

Tahiri met Luke's eyes with her large green ones. "Yes, we got lost. We were so frightened," she said. Tahiri looked like she was going to cry.

Luke shook his head. "I'm sorry that you were lost, but there is no excuse for sneaking out of the academy. I should punish you both," Luke said sadly.

"Please give us another chance, Uncle Luke," Anakin begged. "We will never sneak away again," he promised.

"Please, Master Luke, don't punish Anakin. It was all my fault," Tahiri cried. Tahiri ignored Anakin's look of confusion and kept talking. "I just had to go out to see the jungle. I've never seen a jungle before. I've never seen so much water. I talked Anakin into coming with me because I was afraid to go there alone."

Luke looked at the young girl. He could understand her desire to see the jungle—he had grown up on the desert planet of Tatooine, too. But that was still no excuse.

"Uncle Luke, it's my fault, too," Anakin said softly. His eyes met Luke's. "I chose to go with Tahiri. I'm responsible for my choices."

Tahiri couldn't help letting a small smile cross

her lips. Anakin had finally said he was responsible for his choices. It wasn't that she was happy that he was sharing the blame; she'd expected Anakin to do that. It was that he had taken a step toward understanding that he had the power to make his own choices. That meant he had the power to choose to use the Force for good. Anakin didn't have to be like his grandfather Darth Vader if he didn't choose to be.

Luke turned toward Tahiri. He had seen her smile. Luke was surprised to see that the young girl also understood that Anakin had difficulty recognizing that he could make his own choices. Luke, Leia, and Han had known for some time that the boy believed he might turn out to be like his grandfather. Perhaps, Luke thought, Leia shouldn't have named her son Anakin. After all, Anakin Skywalker was a difficult man to come to understand. This had been true even for Luke.

So much wisdom in a child so young, Luke thought as he stared at Tahiri. The girl was a mess. Her hair was full of leaves and small twigs. Her orange jumpsuit was soaked through. And her bare feet were covered with mud. But so much wisdom, Luke thought in amazement.

Luke Skywalker closed his eyes. He knew in his heart that Anakin Solo was meant to be a powerful Jedi. He would serve the light side of the Force well, once he understood completely that Darth Vader's choices had nothing to do with his own.

And the younger one, Tahiri, continued to surprise Luke. On Tatooine he had thought she was strong in the Force. But he had not imagined the extent of the strength and power that lay deep within her. There was also a strange connection between the two students. Alone they were powerful. But together they could make a stronger unit than many adult Jedi teams. Luke felt that Tahiri and Anakin were meant to train together, that perhaps in the future they would serve the Force as a team.

Luke Skywalker opened his eyes and stared at his students. He could not end their chance to become Jedi because of one foolish action. "This can never happen again," he warned them. "Now go to your rooms and sleep. We will discuss this further tomorrow." Anakin, Tahiri, and Artoo moved slowly into the Temple.

"Where's Ikrit?" Tahiri whispered to her friend.

"I don't know. I guess he ran off into the jungle," Anakin whispered back.

That night Anakin couldn't sleep. What did all of it mean? he wondered. What was he and Tahiri's destiny? How could they figure out the secret of the golden globe? And what was that strange voice that spoke sometimes in his head? Why did it tell him that he couldn't share his secrets with Uncle Luke?

Anakin's thoughts were interrupted by a scratching at the stones of his window. He turned and saw Ikrit. "Hey, friend, how'd you find me?" Anakin asked the little white creature as he motioned it inside his room. Ikrit leapt onto his bed and began to snuggle under the covers. "Hey, that's not your bed," Anakin said to the creature. "If you want to stay that's fine, but not in my bed!" Ikrit snuggled down farther, its large floppy ears resting on Anakin's pillow. "Great, just great," Anakin muttered. "Now I've lost my bed to a furry jungle creature."

"Watch who you call a jungle creature," a scratchy voice said. It was the same strange voice that Anakin had been hearing in his head. Only this time it came from the being in his bed.

SIXTEEN

"You spoke!" Anakin said in surprise.

"I thought you wanted to know where the strange voice in your head was coming from," Ikrit replied, its blue eyes boring into Anakin's. "Well, here it is."

Anakin moved over to the edge of his bed and sat down. Tahiri is never going to believe this, he thought.

"Yes she will," Ikrit replied.

"You read my thoughts," Anakin cried.

"Right again," Ikrit said with a snickering laugh.

"Who are you, and why have you been talking to me inside my head?" Anakin demanded. "And why were you sleeping by the golden globe? Do you know what the globe is?"

"If you stop asking questions I will tell you everything I know," Ikrit replied. Anakin fell silent.

"My name is Ikrit. I am an ancient Jedi Master. I came to Yavin 4 four hundred years ago to study the ruins of the Massassi temples. I discovered the golden globe. There is a curse that surrounds the globe. A curse that I cannot break. So I curled up at the base of the globe to wait for the people who *could* break it. Those people are you and your friend Tahiri." Ikrit stopped speaking and snuggled beneath the covers of Anakin's bed. It seemed that he was done talking.

"I have a lot of questions," Anakin said slowly.

"Then ask them," Ikrit replied.

"Why Tahiri and me?" Anakin began.

"Because you are the ones who can break the curse. That is why I brought you to the Palace of the Woolamander. And I was right about you both, because together your strength in the Force allowed you to unlock the door that led to the golden globe," Ikrit replied.

"What is the globe?" Anakin asked.

"I cannot tell you that, for I do not know for certain—although I have my ideas. I can only say that the spirits of thousands depend on your finding the answer to that question," Ikrit answered. "And I only know that because I *feel* it, deep within my old bones."

"But what about the curse, then? What exactly is it?" Anakin asked.

Ikrit shook his head again. "I do not know or I

would have tried to break it. That is a question you must answer for yourself."

"Why can't I ask my uncle Luke for help? After all, he's a Jedi Master," Anakin said.

"He is an adult. An adult cannot break the curse or I would have done it myself," Ikrit said with a scowl. "If you tell Luke Skywalker, the golden globe will explode into a million pieces of crystal and everything will be lost," Ikrit warned. "I know this, too, only from a feeling. A deep, terrible, unmistakable feeling of dread."

"*What* will be lost?" Anakin cried.

"You know the answer to that," the Jedi Master said softly.

"The children Tahiri and I saw and heard inside the globe," Anakin whispered. "The children will be lost. But what children? Who are they, and how can Tahiri and I possibly save them?"

Ikrit shook his head. "I grow impatient with you, young Anakin. I would not have led you and Tahiri to the Palace of the Woolamander if you did not have the power to understand and break the curse. That means you also have the power to save the children. The only question I have for you is this: Will you answer the call? Will you attempt to break the curse and save the children?"

Anakin met Ikrit's large eyes. He knew that he had to talk to Tahiri about this. He had to tell her everything Ikrit had said to him. They would make this decision together—as a team.

But Anakin already knew what that decision would be: He and Tahiri would help. What else could they do? He knew that it would take all of their combined strength and the power of the Force to solve the mystery of the golden globe and save those trapped inside its crystal.

Anakin heard Luke Skywalker's words from that first school assembly. "The Jedi Code: A Jedi's promise must be the most serious, the deepest of his or her life. A Jedi seeks not adventure or excitement, for a Jedi is passive, calm, and at peace. A Jedi knows that anger, fear, and aggression lead to the dark side. A Jedi uses the Force for knowledge and defense, never for attack. There is no 'try,' only 'do.' Believe and you succeed. Above all else, know that control of the Force comes only from concentration and training." Yes, there could be no other decision but to work as a team with Tahiri and break the curse, Anakin thought.

"Then may the Force be with you and Tahiri, young Anakin," Ikrit said softly. "For you have chosen a difficult path."

The Force is very strong with Anakin—and
his uncle Luke thinks it's time for him
to start his training . . .

STAR WARS
Junior Jedi Knights

Anakin and Tahiri are off on an adventure to the distant moon of Yavin 8! But they are in for a big surprise. Deep within the caves of Lyric's world are carvings that match the ones they found back in the temple on Yavin 4. If they can read them, they might be able to break the curse of the mysterious Golden Globe and defeat the dark side of the Force!

But there is something waiting for them down in the caves. Something large and dangerous. And it will take more than the Force to defeat it!

Turn the page for a special preview of the next book
in the
STAR WARS: JUNIOR JEDI KNIGHTS series:
LYRIC'S WORLD
Coming in January from Boulevard Books!

Barely a moment later, the ear-shattering shriek of an avril rolled down over the group. Anakin didn't have to ask what the creature was. He felt its enormous shadow fall across his back before he looked up to see blood red talons slashing down toward the group. The Melodies quickly formed a circle and began to heave stones up at the creature. Several hit, but only maddened the black bird. Tahiri grabbed a large rock and threw it, hard. Her shot struck the avril directly between the eyes. It shrieked in anger and dove toward her, beak open, talons outstretched. Tahiri dodged, but not before one of its massive wings struck and threw her meters away from the group.

Anakin raced over to protect his friend. But he wasn't quick enough. The avril dove toward Tahiri, talons outstretched, its scream of attack mingling with her cry of terror. Anakin was too far away to reach her, and dread washed over him in an icy cold wave. A split second before Tahiri was swept away in the avril's hungry grasp, Lyric, who was closest to her, leapt forward. She threw her body over Tahiri's to shield her friend. The avril sank his talons into the orange academy jumpsuit Lyric wore, and shot toward the sky. Lyric hung limply in the air.

All who stood helpless on the tundra of the moon could see the look of terror on Lyric's face as she was borne away.

"Where is it taking her?" Tahiri cried. Both she and Anakin whirled to face the Melodies.

"There is nothing to be done," one of the young boys said sadly. "It will take her to its nest and she will be gone before we can ever reach it."

"But she's survived before," Anakin said.

"Yes, but this time she is too weak, she is ready for the changing. If she is not in the waters of the cove before sunrise, she will die," the boy replied.

"Where's the nest?" Anakin asked in a voice that couldn't be argued with. The boy pointed to a spot halfway up the mountain, and Anakin and Tahiri raced toward it. "Be here when we return to take us to the cove," Anakin called over his shoulder.

They'd been climbing for over an hour. Anakin could hear the rasp of his breath, the thundering of his heart. Tahiri was right behind him. She, too, was gasping. There was less oxygen in the air because of the altitude, and several times Anakin had felt dizzy, felt black walls threatening to close out his consciousness, and he'd turned around to make sure Tahiri was still on her feet. They didn't speak as they climbed. Instead they focused on the dark hole where the young Melodie had pointed. Believe and you succeed, Anakin thought as he climbed. That was part of the Jedi Code. Anakin repeated it over and over in his head. He saw the purplish rocks beneath his scraped hands begin to lighten as dawn threatened to cover the moon in its soft glow. Anakin climbed faster.

They stopped five meters from the entrance to the avril's nest. Anakin could hear the creature shrieking within the shallow cave. He and Tahiri crept forward, trying not to dislodge any rocks. They didn't want the bird to know they were there. Carefully they moved toward the opening, peeking around rocks until they were directly below the cave. Anakin raised himself up slowly and peered into the dimly lit cavern. He smelled the foul air and heard the rustling and chirping of the creature's chicks before his eyes grew used to the cave. Then he saw Lyric.

She was alive. Her body hung over the edge of the avril's nest, ringlets of red hair reaching down to the ground. As she had done before, she was chirping, weakly, trying to sound like the mottled black chicks around her. Anakin could hear Lyric struggling for the breath she needed to make the noises. She could barely gasp out the sounds. Still, her efforts had been enough to confuse the creature, whose black head was cocked to one side. But Lyric's efforts were not enough to send the avril out looking for more food. Anakin crouched back down and crawled over to Tahiri.

"I've got to go in there," Anakin mouthed to his friend. A look of alarm spread across Tahiri's features. "I'm going to try to get the avril to leave her nest to search for more food."

"I'm going too," Tahiri mouthed back.

"No, stay hidden in the rocks. I might need your help, or Lyric might. It won't do us any good if the avril attacks us both," Anakin whispered furiously.

"I don't like this," Tahiri mouthed with a scowl.

Anakin turned and crept back up to the nest. Then he let out a shriek. The avril burst out of the cave and loomed above him,

her beak open wide in an ear-shattering cry. Anakin stood fast
and shrieked again, in what he hoped was the sound of one of
the creature's chicks. He saw the bird's beady eyes boring down
on him. And when the avril rushed forward, he was struck by
foul, sour air. With a swift motion, the bird grasped him in its
beak and flung him into her nest. Anakin curled into a ball next
to the chicks and continued to shriek. The avril began to hop
from foot to foot, wings flapping in distress.

That's right, Anakin thought, I'm not dinner. Go out and find
some food for your hungry babies. Lyric continued to chirp and
attempted a shriek, but her lungs couldn't sustain the effort.
Then, with a sudden burst, the avril left her nest and soared
away from the mountain.

"Anakin, are you all right?" Tahiri called as she scrambled to
the opening of the cave.

"I'm fine," Anakin replied. "But Lyric's in bad shape. We've
got to get her out of here."

Tahiri wrinkled her nose as the thick, dank smell of the cave
struck her. Then she climbed into the nest and began to help
Anakin lift Lyric.

"Leave me," Lyric gasped. "It's too late. Save yourselves. The
avril will be back soon."

"There is no try, only do," Tahiri muttered under her breath
as she hoisted one of Lyric's arms over her shoulders. Anakin
lifted the other one. As they dragged their friend from the
avril's nest, both Anakin and Tahiri saw the symbols carved in
the purple rocks. "This is the same place she was taken before,"
Tahiri gasped in surprise.

"We'd better hurry," Anakin said. They quickly left the cave
and began the journey down the mountain. At times Lyric tried
to help her friends carry her, but her efforts didn't last long.
Movement made it too difficult for her to breathe. Finally,
Anakin hoisted Lyric onto his back. He listened to her wheezing
breaths in his ear as he carried her. Tahiri scrambled down the
rocks in front of him, then helped him keep his balance as he
climbed down. They were running out of time. Suddenly they
heard the maddened scream of the avril overhead.

"Over here," a boy's voice called. Anakin saw the young Melodie he'd told to wait. With renewed energy, he moved quickly over to the boy. Several more Melodies were waiting, and they lifted Lyric off Anakin's back and carried her through a small hole in the rocks. The avril landed by the hole and shrieked angrily. It was too small for her to follow her prey. Anakin, Tahiri, and the Melodies heard the creature scraping at the rocks with her talons. Her scrapes and cries faded into the distance as the group raced through a tunnel in the mountain.

Anakin and Tahiri followed the Melodies. The tunnel within the purple mountain of Sistra wound deep, and just when Anakin began to fear that Lyric would run out of time before they reached the cove, the afternoon light began to pour toward the group. They reached an opening, and before them was a circular area, roughly ten meters round, filled with water that was blanketed with blue green algae. The Melodies who carried Lyric moved toward the edge of the pool and gently slid Lyric in. She floated on the bed of algae for a moment, then slowly sank beneath it and disappeared from view.

Tahiri and Anakin stared at the blue green pool of water. It rippled with movement from beneath its surface. Anakin turned and studied the cove. It was set deep within the mountain, but the jagged rocks that ringed it did not close out the sky. The entire cove was open to a shaft of thick sunlight. Perched on the rocks surrounding the pool were young Melodies with bagsful of stones.

"She'll be all right now," one of the Melodies said in a voice that sounded like the soft patter of water falling on dry sand. "You brought her in time."